'I don't play g

Paul shrugged. '
It's in the chemist.y.

'I don't believe that,' Miranda replied.

'You really are dangerously naïve,' he told her. Turning her face up to his, he looked at her searchingly. Miranda withstood it with what composure she could manage.

'You're going to tell me all about love, are you, little one?' Paul said with a softness that even Miranda realised was dangerous.

Dear Reader

Here we are once again at the end of the year... looking forward to Christmas and to the delightful surprises the new year holds. During the festivities, though, make sure you let Mills & Boon help you to enjoy a few precious hours of escape. For, with our latest selection of books, you can meet the men of your dreams and travel to far-away places—without leaving the comfort of your own fireside!

Till next month,

The Editor

Born in London, **Sophie Weston** is a traveller by nature who started writing when she was five. She wrote her first romance recovering from illness, thinking her travelling was over. She was wrong, but she enjoyed it so much that she has carried on. These days she lives in the heart of the city with two demanding cats and a cherry tree—and travels the world looking for settings for her stories.

Recent titles by the same author:

TRIUMPH OF THE DAWN
ICE AT HEART

SAVING THE DEVIL

BY
SOPHIE WESTON

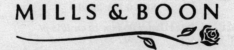

MILLS & BOON LIMITED
ETON HOUSE, 18-24 PARADISE ROAD
RICHMOND, SURREY TW9 1SR

DID YOU PURCHASE THIS BOOK WITHOUT A COVER?

If you did, you should be aware it is **stolen property** as it was reported *unsold and destroyed* by a retailer. Neither the Author nor the publisher has received any payment for this book.

All the characters in this book have no existence outside the imagination of the Author, and have no relation whatsoever to anyone bearing the same name or names. They are not even distantly inspired by any individual known or unknown to the Author, and all the incidents are pure invention.

All Rights Reserved. The text of this publication or any part thereof may not be reproduced or transmitted in any form or by any means, electronic or mechanical, including photocopying, recording, storage in an information retrieval system, or otherwise, without the written permission of the publisher.

This book is sold subject to the condition that it shall not, by way of trade or otherwise, be lent, resold, hired out or otherwise circulated without the prior consent of the publisher in any form of binding or cover other than that in which it is published and without a similar condition including this condition being imposed on the subsequent purchaser.

MILLS & BOON and the Rose Device are trademarks of the publisher.

First published in Great Britain 1994 by Mills & Boon Limited

© Sophie Weston 1994

Australian copyright 1994   Philippine copyright 1994 This edition 1994

ISBN 0 263 78769 9

Set in Times Roman 10 on 10½ pt. 01-9412-58743 C

Made and printed in Great Britain

CHAPTER ONE

THE wind shook the shutters like an angry giant fist. Miranda hugged her arms, trying to convince herself that she wasn't afraid.

'Adventure,' she said aloud, although there was no one else in the small house to hear her. 'That's what you said you wanted, my girl. Now it's here. Pull yourself together and enjoy it.'

The wind moaned again and there was another of those ominous cracking noises. Miranda thought of the huge trees that formed the jungle around the small clearing and winced. There was the unmistakable sound of another torn branch hitting the ground. How long before one of the falling limbs fell through the simple corrugated-iron roof?

If only her father would come. He had left early yesterday morning, brushing away Miranda's anxious reminder about the storm warning. He had been planning his trip upriver for months. Now that the boat was loaded with provisions and the specially translated bibles he wasn't to be deflected. Not by considerations of personal safety. Not by the claims of a worried daughter.

The shutters banged and shook with sudden violence. Something touched her ankle. Miranda jumped. Five years in the jungle had taught her to be careful of small things that touched lightly clad skin. She looked down in quick alarm.

It was of brief duration. She met the uncertainly focused eyes of one of the new kittens. She gave a slightly ragged laugh and scooped the little creature up.

'Hello, sweet. Got left behind?' she said.

Mia, the mission cat, had been transferring her kittens from the outhouse to some unknown destination up the hillside all day. It was one of the signs, João had told her, that a bad storm was coming. The animals knew and made for high ground.

The kitten seemed unaware that it had been abandoned. It snuggled under Miranda's chin, its small claws working in the stuff of her jacket. It began to purr.

'I'm glad you're comfortable,' Miranda said drily.

But she didn't dislodge it. In fact it was oddly comforting. She tickled it absent-mindedly as she went through the house.

It was dark. That wasn't entirely due to the strange storm light outside. On João's instructions she had closed and battened the shutters before he left. She had shut off the Calor gas supply as well, in case of fire, and lit a couple of candles. Their flames shivered and nearly went out from time to time as the house shook. It was not, thought Miranda wryly, reassuring.

'You will be all right,' João had said. He hadn't sounded convinced. But by that time he had stayed as long as he could—and longer than anyone else at the mission. He had a family to care for in their exposed settlement downriver. Miranda had been urging him to go back to them for several hours.

'Of course I will,' she said. 'The mission was built here because it's sheltered. Nothing will happen to me, João. We've had bad storms before.'

And they had. In the five years since she had been with her father, there had been high winds, thunderstorms that had sent thirty-foot trees crashing, and rains that had turned the yellow paths to mud. She had survived it all, battening down the roof and conserving food and power—while her father had ignored the danger and talked of the sanctity of his mission, she remembered. But she didn't remember a storm that had sounded like this one.

The radio was dead. It had died that afternoon before João left. He had fiddled with it, clearly more and more worried, but he hadn't been able to find out what was wrong. When Miranda had finally persuaded him to set off for home, he had only done so with the promise of sending someone to repair it. As the winds grew higher and the more branches fell, Miranda thought there wasn't much hope of that now.

'So it's just you and me,' she said to the kitten.

She peered out through the crack in the shutters. The path up from the village was running with water. Only an hour ago it had been still, visibly a path, albeit one with numerous large puddles. Now it looked like a small stream, the water tumbling continually down to the river.

Miranda straightened, biting her lip. She had seen the phenomenon before. It had never got so bad so quickly, though, in her experience. And she had never been in the mission house on her own before. If her father hadn't been there—and most of the time he hadn't—one of the mission workers had taken charge.

She knew what she ought to do, of course. Dress properly against the elements, take a small backpack of essential supplies, and make for high ground before the Rio Verde broke its banks. The trouble was that in a storm of this violence all the tracks she knew through the forest would be awash and probably impassable. And she wasn't sufficiently skilled to make her way through the virgin rainforest beyond the native pathways.

'What do you think?' she asked the kitten drily. 'Drown here at home? Or risk starvation and snake-bite and God knows how many months of being lost in the rainforest?'

The kitten closed its eyes, unmoved.

'Thank you very much for your considered advice,' said Miranda.

But she tickled it behind the ear and felt a bit better. The nasty little flicker of panic was dying. Panic, she knew, was a much surer killer than either the muddy waters of the Amazon tributary or the forest itself.

'Well, there's no point in dancing from foot to foot, talking to the livestock,' Miranda said to herself aloud.

'The storm may pass but it doesn't look like it. The thing to do is get ready to leave. Just in case.'

It wasn't difficult. There was a small knapsack kept ready anyway, in case of emergency calls for what little first aid the mission could provide. She checked through its contents, while the kitten clung to her shoulder.

It was all there: dried food, vitamins, water purification tablets, rudimentary utensils. She extracted most of the medical supplies. She was more likely to need additional food than aspirin, Miranda thought wryly.

She knew what to wear. She had had it drummed into her the first week she arrived. The American anthropologist had still been there then.

Her father had been furious that Rolf Pulos had marched her into the forest, showing her what to wear and what to watch and how to find her way among the giant tree trunks when the sky was hidden by the forest canopy. He had shown her how to use the compass too and the oddest map she had ever seen, roughly drawn on oiled cloth.

Harry, Miranda remembered wryly, had been faintly disapproving of the walk. And outraged, for some reason, by the map.

'The work of the devil,' he had spat, wrenching it away from Pulos.

The American had raised his eyebrows. 'It's a damned good map. The man's a professional.'

Henry Lane had looked as ferocious as Miranda had ever seen him. 'A professional seducer.'

Pulos had looked amused. It must have been that which goaded Henry into vituperation. Normally he'd guarded his temper in front of Miranda in those days.

'He only owns that place because his father's family had to pay him off to leave Rio. He may lecture all round the world on that so-called research of his but he only came north because his family won't acknowledge him any more. He's a wicked man.'

Pulos had shrugged. 'He makes a good map, though.'

Henry had opened his mouth to retort, then seemed to think better of it. He turned his attention back to Miranda.

'You're not a tourist. You're here to work. The mission paid your fare, you know. You owe them, even if you won't do God's proper work.'

It had become an immediate source of conflict, that refusal of hers to join him in his preaching. He seemed as if he could not accept it. In the end he'd barely spoken to her except about practical matters.

She sighed now, thinking of it. No, it wasn't much of a relationship and it wasn't going to be, for all her hopes when she came out to Brazil. Henry Lane was a man obsessed. He was ready to exploit anyone in pursuit of that work. The hard-working mission teachers, the desperately poor local villagers, the passing Indian scouts—he used them all. Why should he treat his daughter any differently?

Miranda shut off that line of thought abruptly. It led to nothing except self-pity. She had taken a risk, deciding to accept her father's invitation to join him. She had known it was a risk and everyone had warned her. But she had let her curiosity win. Curiosity, she knew, and the orphan's deeply buried desire for someone of her own. Well, she had taken the risk and it had taught her a lot, not least that affection was not an automatic accompaniment to family relations.

It was, she thought now, a mistake she wouldn't make again. After all, she had lived without love for most of her life and survived. She didn't need it. And she wasn't going to risk any more hurt by chasing that particular rainbow again.

'If, of course,' she said aloud, 'I ever get out of this place. Or even survive the night,' she added as a particularly loud crash announced that another branch had fallen dangerously close to the house.

She detached the kitten. It curled up on the pillow of her narrow truckle bed as she stripped off her jeans. The material soaked up moisture and retained it, Rolf had told her. What she needed for the jungle was maximum cover in natural fibres. She found cotton trousers, a silk shirt and scarf, cotton safari jacket and long cotton socks. She pulled on the shirt and trousers, debating.

She had to wear high boots, of course, in case she had to wade through infested waters. If she had to go into the rainforest that seemed an all too likely probability. They weren't comfortable and she didn't like them but they were better than blood-sucking insects, she reminded herself. She struggled into them, cursing.

'And now what?' she said, standing up. 'Fresh water, of course. A knife, I suppose. What else?'

She caught sight of herself in the mirror that João, ignoring her father's disapproval, had brought as a birthday present from the mission teachers last year. It was a disreputable picture. Miranda grinned and faced up to herself.

She saw a tall, whip-thin figure, pale in the shadows. Her unremarkable brown hair had grown long and silky. She wore it caught back in a plait when she taught but now it was loose and wildly disarranged. She flicked a lock disparagingly.

'If it weren't for that,' she told her image, 'you could be a boy. In fact you look like a pirate.'

She put her hands on her hips and swaggered at her image. The boots were thigh-high, making her legs look impossibly long and slender. The loose sleeves of the silk shirt billowed. Suddenly she laughed aloud.

'Errol Flynn, eat your heart out,' she said cheerfully.

The kitten raised its head and mewed.

Instantly she was rueful. 'I suppose you're hungry,' she said.

The kittens were lapping now, so the little animal wouldn't starve if it was separated from its mother. It was pretty clear that Mia wasn't coming back for her last child, so that was just as well.

'Poor little orphan,' said Miranda. 'You and I have a lot in common, fluffball.' She pulled its ears gently and it began to purr. 'If I have to go I'll leave you some food,' she said, to reassure herself rather than the cat. 'There isn't much I can do about your family. I expect they'll come back and find you when the storm is over, though.'

But the awakened cat seemed to know that something new was happening. It took some of the food she gave it but, the moment she moved back into her bedroom, left its dish to follow her.

'This,' said Miranda, searching under the kitten's suspicious eye for a hat to confine her hair, 'could be difficult.'

The wind was howling continuously now. Miranda could see through the chinks in the shutters that the path was now a crawling stream of mud. There wasn't much time if she was going to be able to get out of the clearing and up on to higher ground.

She plaited her hair and pinned it up swiftly, pulling the waxed-cotton hat down over it. The kitten mewed. She took it back to its dish. It ignored it and came back to her, plucking at her boots with tiny claws.

She picked it up, stroking it.

'You won't like it out there, Orphan Annie,' she said. 'It's wet and windy and it's going to get horribly cold tonight. You'll be warmer here. And probably safer.'

The cat stuffed its head under her chin. Miranda sighed.

'And on your own,' she said. 'Yes, I know. Oh, all right; you win. You'll probably get lost and I'm sure I don't know how to take care of you in the jungle. But I'll have a go. Orphans should stick together, I suppose.'

She pulled on a jerkin and then the waxed-cotton jacket that would keep out most of the rain. Inside she was shaking with fear. She had lived in the rainforest long enough to hear the tales of unaccustomed visitors who went into the trees and were never seen again.

She had never felt so alone, Miranda thought. And hers had not been a life full of companionship. She belted the jacket determinedly, trying not to think about it. If only her father hadn't insisted on going off upriver. If only he had come back when the storm got up. If only she hadn't come to Brazil in the first place looking for God knew what—reassurance, a home, love...

'Well, that was a mistake,' Miranda said aloud. 'And I *chose* to do that. Maybe I'll have better luck in the rainforest.'

She checked the long, leather-sheathed forest knife and attached it to her belt. Then she took the compass from the shelf below the wallchart of the American continent. She opened the box, turning the thing carefully. The needle wobbled. Miranda sighed. This, she realised, was the moment of decision. She could sit down, take off her jacket and hat and wait for the storm to increase. Or she could summon up her courage and do what she knew was the sensible thing by making for higher ground.

With cat, she added to herself drily.

But there wasn't really a decision to be made. If she wanted to survive she had to move, she knew. And move fast.

She looked round for a means of carrying the cat. A sling was probably the best, round her neck inside the jacket.

'You'll keep me warm,' she told the kitten. 'Not that that's usually much of a problem.'

Normally the temperature was high enough for only the lightest clothes to be needed, though it could get chilly at night. And indeed the day's coldness this morning had been one of the signs that had set João eyeing the sky anxiously.

The cat settled happily enough in its pouch. Miranda tickled the top of its head absently.

'If only there were a map...' she said.

And then she remembered the map that Harry had almost torn out of the young anthropologist's hands all those years ago. The work of the devil, he had called it, though Miranda had never been able to discover why. Probably, she thought, sighing, because it showed some Indian holy places. Harry was not tolerant of other people's beliefs, especially people he was employed to convert.

Without much hope, Miranda ran her hands along the shelf of books they used for teaching geography. She hadn't seen the map for nearly five years, after all. And if Harry disapproved of it so badly, he had probably destroyed it long ago.

So she could hardly believe her luck when her fingers dislodged a small plastic folder and a number of sketch maps fell out as it dropped squashily to the floor. She crouched among the papers. Most of them were rough and highly imaginative: the children's classwork, she deduced. But a couple were more than that. And one, on rubbed cloth, was neither amateur nor imaginative.

She sat back on her heels, drawing a long breath. Yes, as she remembered, it had compass points and trails marked.

'Maybe the luck is turning our way at last,' she said to the kitten. 'That is if we want to go to——' she turned the map round, inspecting it '—Oachacoa or Ladeira or Fazenda Branco.'

She stopped as a faint memory stirred.

'Branco,' she said thoughtfully.

But it danced tantalisingly at the edge of her memory. Miranda knew that she had heard of the Fazenda Branco but she could not remember where or what she had heard about it. Or even who had spoken of it. Though she was fairly sure it wasn't her father.

She looked at the map again. By local standards it wasn't that far. If it was a farm, as its name suggested, or some other sort of settlement, she would have expected to have met people from there in normal circumstances. Only the mission under Harry's rigorous guidance was not normal, she thought regretfully. Harry had no time for people who weren't willing to listen to his evangelism. And he could be downright unneighbourly to those with rival convictions, as the Franciscan brothers from Nuevo Cavoeiro had found.

'So maybe if I get there they won't welcome me anyway,' Miranda said aloud.

But she didn't really believe it. In this sort of storm nobody would turn a stranger away; even Harry wouldn't. And in general the local people she had met were more hospitable than Harry.

She straightened, replacing the map carefully in its small plastic envelope. She checked that the kitten was secure. Then, with her knees trembling, she made herself fill the two water bottles attached to her pack. There would be plenty of water in the forest, she knew, too much indeed for comfortable travelling, but there was no way of telling whether it was sweet. The purification tablets tasted vile. So at least she could start off with a supply of reasonable-tasting drinking water.

There was another crash, louder and more echoing than any of the others. Miranda jumped and swallowed hard. There was no disguising from herself that, for all her brave preparations, she was very scared indeed.

The kitten awoke and put a protesting paw out of its sling and up the front of her jerkin.

'Don't you start to be a back-seat driver,' she told it in a scolding voice. She noticed that her voice trembled and was angry with herself. 'Panicking isn't going to help,' she said aloud.

The echoes from the last crash were still reverberating. In fact they sounded eerily like human voices.

'Now don't start to fantasise about rescue,' Miranda told herself, swinging the pack on to her back. 'Nobody's going to get you out of this but you.'

The illusion of voices grew stronger.

'Oh, lord, I'm hallucinating. And I haven't even been bitten by anything yet,' Miranda said in disgust. 'Come on, Miranda. One foot in front of the other until you're out there in the lovely rain. The sooner you start, the sooner you'll get somewhere safe. And stop *panicking*.'

She checked the map and the compass and pocketed them before pulling on her gloves and drawing her deepest breath yet.

The old wooden door to the porch banged back on its hinges. The candle-flame lurched wildly. In spite of her instructions to herself, Miranda jumped back with an involuntary scream. The illusion got worse.

'...downstream days ago,' said a crisp, impatient voice. It was a masculine voice, deep and commanding. Even when it wasn't impatient, it sounded like a voice used to giving orders. 'Even that old lunatic wouldn't stay with a hurricane warning out.'

Miranda couldn't make out a reply. She shrank back, fearful that the owner of that imperious voice would appear in the doorway; even more fearful that her jangled senses were playing her false and there was no one there at all.

A quick, firm step and the schoolroom door was thrust open. Miranda retreated, her hand going instinctively to the knife in her belt.

A man appeared in the doorway. He was tall and made to look taller by the crazy shadows. He was looking over his shoulder, talking to someone behind him.

'There's a light but...' He turned back and his eyes found her. 'Good God,' he said blankly. 'Who the hell are you?'

It was barked out like an accusation. He spoke in Portuguese, of course. Miranda decided she didn't like his tone. She straightened her shoulders.

'Henry Lane——' she began but was interrupted.

'Good God, the old fool *is* still here.' He turned on one booted heel and shouted into the small hallway, 'Heitor, you were right. There's a boy. Come in here.'

A *boy*? It took Miranda a second or two to realise that the arrogant stranger was talking about herself. She was still mastering this startling discovery when the tall man's companion arrived. He was shorter and older and distinctly worried.

'Nobody in the bedrooms,' the newcomer said. 'Where's your master, boy?' he added to her. In contrast to the other, his voice was quite kindly.

'Harry—Mr Lane went upriver yesterday,' she muttered. 'On a crusade.'

The man called Heitor looked even more worried. He turned to the other.

'He does these journeys three or four times a year. Calls them "the crusade for the people". Takes the steamer and goes to the settlements preaching and handing out bibles. Usually he sticks to the Rio Verde but if he went up one of the tributaries... Do you know where he was going, boy?'

Miranda knew exactly where her father was going. He was intending to take the boat further into the hinterland than he ever had before. That was why he had been so impatient of delay. He had been working himself up to this, his most dangerous attempt to save heathen souls, for years.

'A settlement called Amaral,' she said huskily. 'He was going to go to an Indian village from there.'

'Amaral!' Heitor looked appalled.

The tall man swore long and fluently.

'When did he go?' he shot at her.

Miranda could feel herself beginning to tremble again. She clenched her gloved fingers into her palm to try to stop it.

'Yesterday morning.'

'Alone?'

She shook her head. 'Rubem Monteiro and his brother were sailing the boat. And he was picking up Lotte Meyer.'

'The German missionary at the miners' camp,' Heitor supplied as the tall man turned a face of angry enquiry to him. 'She's a qualified doctor. She does good work, Paul.'

It sounded, thought Miranda, as if he was trying to appease him. She decided she liked the man called Paul less and less.

'Is there a radio at Amaral?' he shot out now.

Heitor looked unhappy. 'I don't know. I doubt it.'

Paul turned a piercing gaze on Miranda. 'When did you last hear from Lane?'

'I haven't,' she said simply. 'He doesn't call in. He doesn't care about his own safety, you know.'

Or mine, she might have added. But didn't.

He swore again. 'Well, there's no point in sending out search parties now. The storm's going to get a whole lot worse before it gets better. He could have moored the boat and gone for cover.'

His tone said he thought it unlikely. Remembering her father's single-mindedness, so did Miranda. She wondered how the man Paul, whom she had never met before or heard her father speak of, came to know him so well.

His eyes bored into hers.

'Where's everyone else? The children?'

'We sent them home as soon as the storm warnings started.'

Her father had been furious about that. He'd said it set a bad example by mistrusting God's grace. But Miranda had been adamant. And Harry had listened to her, as he was finding that he had to more and more recently, she thought wryly.

'Thank God for that at least. The others?'

'Went yesterday. Except João Montes. I made him go about three hours ago.'

Heitor said swiftly, 'It was Montes I saw at the school. He's safe enough.'

Miranda heaved a sigh of relief. She hadn't realised how worried she had been about the too conscientious João.

'So it's just you. What am I going to do with you?'

Paul looked her up and down unflatteringly. Of course, he didn't realise she was a girl, Miranda reminded herself, enduring it. But even so the cool superiority was unbearable. She closed her lips firmly over a sharp retort. After all, he was probably going to be her escape route.

She said, 'I thought I'd make for higher ground.'

His eyes narrowed, taking in the pack and the outdoor gear for the first time, it seemed.

'Where on higher ground?' he demanded.

He was evidently amused. She set her teeth and replied woodenly, 'I don't really know. I just thought—up. I've got a map and a compass,' she added with a flash of defiance.

The amusement became suddenly complicated. His face stilled. Miranda realised suddenly that it was an outrageously handsome face, thin and expressive with long-lashed dark eyes and a mouth that looked as if it knew all the sensual secrets of the world. She gave a little gasp at her thoughts and tore her eyes away.

'Have you indeed?' he said softly. 'A map?'

'An anthropologist left it behind. Harry said it was the work of the devil,' she said, her voice low and shaking with tension. 'I found it among old schoolwork.'

She had the feeling he was amused again, though the handsome face didn't change.

'The work of the devil, hmm? I must see this devilish map.'

Heitor said warningly, 'Paul...'

But one hand silenced him with just a touch on the shoulder.

'Show me,' Paul told her softly.

Miranda was puzzled. But she saw no reason not to. After all, the map probably made more sense to him than it did to her. She fumbled it out of her pocket and its plastic covering.

He looked at it for a moment without expression. Then she saw that a muscle was working in his cheek, as if he was in the grip of some strong emotion. But when he gave it back to her his voice was cool.

'Keep it. There aren't too many maps of the rainforest,' he said.

Heitor said again, 'Paul...'

He turned a brilliant smile on his companion, a flash of white teeth in the uncertain shadows.

'We'd better be moving. The wind can only get worse. We'll take the boy with us. When the storm's over we'll find Lane.'

For some reason it sounded like a threat.

Heitor said, 'Take him where?' He sounded wary.

'Back to Fazenda Branco, of course.'

'But——'

'Heitor,' Paul said softly.

The older man shrugged. 'Your horse or mine?'

Miranda said with a certain amount of satisfaction that she knew was petty, 'I can't ride.'

Paul shrugged. 'We'll have to go on foot most of the way anyway. Where we can ride, I'll take him up on Lemanja. She's fresher and she's carried two before. The boy doesn't look much of a weight.'

He spoke as if she weren't there, Miranda thought, enraged. She said cautiously, 'I'm afraid of horses.'

The looks she encountered would have made her laugh in other circumstances. Heitor looked astounded. Paul looked neither surprised nor moved, though she detected a faint curl of his lip.

'I'm sorry for that, young missionary,' he said lightly. 'But you'll have to bear it. Look on it as a trial of the spirit,' he advised, turning away. 'Put that candle out and come.'

Miranda gave a small, furious exclamation before she could stop herself. Heitor had already gone. The man called Paul turned back to her, one eyebrow raised.

'Understand me, boy,' he said softly. 'I'm no friend to missionaries. And Henry Lane and I have a number of scores to settle. You can come with us and co-operate, or you're on your own. Which is it to be?'

Miranda met hard dark eyes with a sense of shock. A little shiver went up her spine. I am not afraid of him, she told herself. I am not afraid of any man in the world. He hasn't got a knife or a gun on me and I don't care what he thinks of me. People can only hurt you if you care about them and I don't.

Outside the wind screamed and the rain sounded like the end of the world. His eyes seemed to will her into submission. To her chagrin, her eyes fell.

'I'll co-operate,' she muttered, dousing the candle.

'Then come,' he said, spinning her round with a none too gentle hand on her shoulder.

Outside was as bad as it had sounded. Heitor was already astride a horse that looked sturdy rather than handsome. It stood placidly enough, in spite of the hellish noise and the drenching it was getting.

Paul's horse was a different matter. She looked huge to Miranda, who was dismayed at the height of the massive shoulders she was supposed to mount. And the horse wouldn't stand still.

Miranda tried to put one foot in the stirrups and haul herself up as she had seen on the movies. It didn't work. The horse backed, snorting, forcing Miranda to hop beside her in an undignified attempt to stay upright.

'Stand still, you damned monster,' she said between her teeth.

'Such language from a missionary,' Paul said disapprovingly.

Miranda swung round, hating him, and nearly lost her balance. How could he have overheard her muttered words with that cacophony above them? He gently detached her imprisoned foot.

'Surely even apprentice missionaries aren't allowed to use words like that?' She glared at him. His amusement grew. 'Or like what you're thinking now,' he added. 'Come on; we haven't got all day. Up with you.'

Miranda found herself tossed unceremoniously into the saddle. She grabbed it, too alarmed to stand on her dignity. It seemed an awful long way to the ground, when she dared to look down. Her hands clenched convulsively on the worn leather of the saddle. The mare moved restlessly, clearly no more comfortable than she was herself.

Miranda looked at her rescuer. The rain had flattened his hair to a sleek black cap. It was running down his face over his jutting brow but he paid no more attention to it than if it were a light drizzle. He was looking up at her with narrowed eyes. For a moment she thought he looked shocked, even angry. But when his eyes met her own, he was laughing. He shook his head.

'What do they teach you boys before they send you out here?' he said in a taunting voice. 'Urban first aid? Don't be scared. Lemanja knows what she's doing even if you don't.'

Miranda was on the point of replying in kind when a small movement in the area of her waist made her break off. She had forgotten the kitten. Now the little animal was stirring. Unobtrusively she plucked at the front of her jacket to give it more air. She was fairly sure that her rescuer was not the sort of man to welcome taking along a feline passenger. So she swallowed her justified anger and said pacifically, 'I've ridden the mule, of course. But before I came here I never had to ride any animal.'

His eyes glinted. 'Sometime you must tell me how the hell you got yourself posted to the rainforest.' He slammed a wide-brimmed hat on his head and took hold of the horse's head and the saddle, bracing himself. 'And how Henry Lane managed to leave you behind.'

He swung himself up behind her and gathered the reins by dint of passing his arms round her. Miranda prevented herself from stiffening only by a supreme effort of will. Instead she huddled down into her disguising jacket and hoped that he would be too intent on the difficult terrain to pay too much attention to what he held in his arms.

He certainly was not paying her any attention now. He wheeled the mare round to come face to face with Heitor.

'Up the escarpment,' he shouted, pointing at the trees to the south. 'I'll lead.'

Heitor nodded. He looked thoroughly miserable under his own brimmed hat. But he didn't protest about Paul's high-handedness. It did not look as if anyone ever protested, Miranda thought resentfully. At least, to judge from the way Paul set off, without waiting for Heitor to signify consent, he didn't expect opposition.

She found herself thinking wistfully of finding some way to spike his guns, so that for once he didn't get his own arrogant way. It was, she acknowledged, extraordinary. Especially as he and Heitor had rescued her from the solitary flight into the unknown forest that she had dreaded.

It didn't make any difference. She detested the man into whose hard arms she was now committed. And she would take any opportunity that was offered to make it plain that she held him in a contemptuous dislike quite equal to that which he evidently felt for her.

In fact Miranda was in a temper greater than any she had ever had in her life before.

CHAPTER TWO

THE ride was a nightmare for Miranda. In very little time her legs were one burning ache from hip to toe. The man gave no sign of being aware of it, however. If she shifted to make her position more comfortable, she was roundly cursed. Apart from that he did not address her.

He and Heitor seemed to communicate without words, too. They took their horses in a twisting scramble through undergrowth and slipping hillside at a rate which would have alarmed Miranda on a calm, sunlit day. In the rain it was terrifying. To begin with, when rocks crashed down the hillside behind them, she jumped and looked round. But Paul wrenched her painfully back into place and after a few times she did so no more.

She lost track of time. The forest was so dark between the tree cover and the stormclouds that she could hardly tell whether it was day or night. And, much as she disliked him, she could only marvel at the sureness with which Paul found their way. Heitor seemed to hesitate sometimes; Paul never.

Eventually he drew rein and let Heitor's mount catch up.

'About an hour to sunset,' he said—not to Miranda.

Heitor looked anxious. He brought a two-way radio out of his saddle-pack and raised the aerial. The forest filled with the sound of static and indecipherable distant gabbling. Somewhere a parrot shrieked. Miranda didn't jump at that. She was used to parrots.

Heitor shook his head, smacking the aerial back into its telescoped position.

'Still too much interference.'

Paul frowned. 'It's about an hour to the ridge.'

Heitor's look of anxiety deepened. 'Paul, I should get back. They will need me when they start bringing in the injured.'

'Will you be able to find your way?'

A faint smile touched the older man's mouth. 'Not like you. But if I keep going up and south-west, I should hit the trail.'

Paul looked at him searchingly. 'And if you don't?'

Heitor shrugged. 'Then I spend the night in the forest. Not for the first time.' He touched his arm. 'Don't worry, my friend. You've taught me all the tricks. I shan't lose myself. And you need to be sure that everything is all right at the *fazenda*.'

Paul said, 'If I could get them on the radio...'

Heitor shook his head. 'There is only one solution and you know it.' He hesitated. 'Do you want me to take the boy?'

It was with a little shock that Miranda realised he was referring to herself. It was also a shock to realise that neither of the men really wanted her.

'No,' Paul was saying. 'He can make himself useful at the *fazenda*. These missionaries are trained paramedics. It's basic stuff but we'll need every extra help we can get.'

Miranda's heart sank. It was true that the mission trained its young acolytes in rudimentary remedial medicine. But she had never gone through that training. She had come out to Brazil too young and her father had never let her leave the settlement for training. Or for any other purpose, she thought wryly. So all she knew about medicine she had learned from her father. She devoutly hoped it was enough.

She hung her head and pretended to ignore their conversation. They were paying no attention to her at all, so it wasn't difficult.

Paul and Heitor did not spend long over the farewells.

'Keep in touch,' Paul said briefly, touching the saddle-pouch which presumably held his own radio.

Heitor's grin was infectious, in spite of the worry and fatigue. You could see, thought Miranda, surprised, that he really liked the other man.

'I'll scream for help if a ten-metre anaconda comes for me,' he agreed, grinning.

Paul laughed. It was an attractive laugh, she noticed, with even more surprise. It was low and warm and it did something peculiar to her pulses.

Ridiculous, she told herself, sitting upright. She was obviously overtired. The man wasn't even laughing with her. As far as he was concerned she might just as well have been a bag of flour.

He certainly said nothing to her as he wheeled his horse and took them up a steep incline. The trees were denser here but also lower. At times he and even Miranda had to duck their heads to avoid low-hanging branches.

It was completely dark now. Paul swung a powerful torch out of his pack and attached it to the front of the saddle. The beam showed the ground they were traversing in a brilliant light but the shadows of the tree trunks were menacing. Miranda could hear small animals squeaking as they rushed for cover. Inside her jacket the kitten stirred and then went mouse-still.

Eventually he stopped and slid to the ground. Miranda looked round. It was a small clearing surrounded by four or five trees. It was obvious that people had stopped here before. The ground was flattened where they had sat and there were ashes where they had lit a fire.

'Why are we stopping?' she asked nervously, looking round at the tall shadows.

'I need some gas,' he mocked. Then, impatiently, 'We rest here. We can't ride all night.'

Miranda swallowed. 'I—that is, you don't need to stop for me. I can carry on.'

His look of amazement said that he not begun to consider her in his decision.

'The mare can't,' he said curtly. 'She's got an added burden in you and it's harder going at night. Get down and make a fire.' As she didn't move he looked at her narrowly. 'You do know how to make a fire, young missionary?'

'Yes,' Miranda said with equal curtness. Five years living on the edge of the forest had taught her most of the basics.

'Then get off and give the poor horse a rest.'

She hated him. 'I don't think I can,' she admitted.

For a moment he stared. Then he gave a heartless crack of laughter.

'I never thought of that. I suppose it's been a hard ride for your first attempt.'

He put his hands up and lifted her down as easily as if she had been a child. It was not very dignified. It was even less dignified when Miranda staggered as soon as his hands left her.

He caught her at once.

'Cramp?' He didn't sound unsympathetic. But Miranda was too taken up with the unexpected failure of her leg muscles to notice. She shook her head, her eyes wide and alarmed.

'No. I don't know. I can't feel my legs properly.'

'Unaccustomed muscles,' he said, lowering her gently to the ground. 'Rub them. The feeling will soon come back.'

Miranda did as she was told. Her slight feeling of resentment dissipated as the blood began to circulate and her legs began to hurt in good earnest. She rocked a little. Paul set up the heavy-duty flashlight on the ground and set about removing the mare's harness. He didn't notice her discomfort. Well, thought Miranda, her resentment flaring again, he'd notice pretty soon when he found he wasn't getting his fire.

The rain was heavier under the diminished tree cover. The kitten, emerging from her jacket, squeaked miserably. Nevertheless it climbed out and down her trembling legs, to squat tidily under a bush to relieve itself, cross-eyed with misery. In spite of her own woes, Miranda laughed.

Paul swung round from his task.

'What——?' He broke off as he caught sight of the cat.

It looked very appealing, its smudgy tabby face concentrating hard as it scrabbled the earth tidily over its waste. Paul was clearly immune to the appeal. He watched the animal dive back into her jacket, squeaking. His expression was thunderous.

'What the hell,' he said quietly, 'is that?'

Miranda cleared her throat. She had some sympathy with his irritation. After all, she had been in two minds about taking the kitten herself.

'It's—er—the mission cat's last kitten. She moved the others. This one got left behind.'

'And you were taking it to her?' he said with a sarcasm that bit. 'Was that why you were ready to leave when we arrived?'

'Of course not,' said Miranda crossly. The kitten was wet and uncomfortable against her silk shirt. 'I—just couldn't bring myself to leave him. As I didn't think I was going to survive either, it didn't seem to make much difference,' she added truthfully.

His face darkened. He opened his mouth, then took in her drooping shoulders. He bit back whatever it was he was going to say. He shrugged. His eyes were suddenly curious.

'Why didn't you think you were going to survive?'

'I didn't know where I was going. I've never slept out in the forest before. In theory I know the things to avoid. But——' It was Miranda's turn to shrug.

He turned back to his task. He swung the packs to the ground and began to open them.

'How long have you been out here?' he asked over his shoulder.

Miranda debated. Normally she never answered questions like that. Normally her father made sure she wasn't asked them. But now was not a normal time. And who could tell whether she would ever see Henry Lane again?

'Five years,' she said at last.

'Five *years*?' He looked up from the pack in blank astonishment. 'Oh, not with Harry, of course.'

'With Harry.'

The dark face showed naked disbelief.

'I don't know the man well but this isn't an over-populated area. I'd have heard if he had a young assistant with him. The traders would have known. Or the miners.'

'No,' she said quietly.

His brows came together in a wicked line. It made him look more imperious and impatient than ever.

'He hid you? Deliberately?'

Once again his eyes travelled over her in that unsettling, insulting way. Miranda could feel the colour rise in her cheeks. She hoped that the fierce light of his torch would disguise it. She swallowed.

'Yes.'

The steep lids hid his eyes suddenly. But nothing hid the derisive slant of that mocking mouth.

'Want to tell me why?' he drawled.

Miranda swallowed. 'It's complicated...'

The eyes lifted abruptly. Under the charged contempt in them, she took an involuntary step back.

'So,' said Paul with a smile like a stiletto, 'am I. Tell me. Or shall I guess? Could it be your age? You can't have been more than a child when you came, if it was five years ago. What were you? Eleven? Twelve?'

In fact she had been eighteen. But as a boy she wouldn't pass for more than eighteen now, she knew. And, since Paul had made the mistake in the first place, Miranda was oddly reluctant to tell him in this dark and lonely place that she was not a boy. She looked down and told him as much of the truth as she was willing to give.

'He—we—kept it quiet. I used to go into the forest when visitors came. The children knew, of course, because I taught them. And the Indians. Nobody else.'

He weighed this, the thin, clever face forbidding in its concentration. He gave her a look that scorched her. Then, with a quick shrug, he turned back to his task and began deftly extracting material from the pack. He did not look at her or address her again.

Miranda watched him helplessly. She had the feeling that somehow she ought to defend herself against some silent accusation. But she did not know how. She did not even know what the accusation was.

At last he began to spread out the contents of his pack. She could see that it was a tent.

'Why?' he said at last, still not looking at her. He seemed absorbed in his work. He sounded as if the question almost bored him. 'Why did he keep you hidden?'

Miranda bit her lip, watching the play of muscles along those arrogant, indifferent shoulders. She shivered. 'Henry Lane is my father,' she said at last quietly.

That stopped his neat unravelling of the tent. He turned his head and she met a look of such blazing fury that she blinked. But at once he was back to raising the tent.

'You astonish me,' he said in a muffled voice, pegging the ground sheet out and dealing competently with the telescopic poles. 'Has he a wife somewhere? Or are you the fruit of sin?'

The mockery was unexpected, undisguised and unkind. Miranda winced.

'Neither,' she said quietly. 'My mother was his wife. She died in Europe. That was when he brought me out here. And that's the reason for the secrecy. She hated the mission and her family were determined to prevent me from coming back to my father. There were battles in the court. I remember them.'

And that was not all she remembered, though she wasn't going to tell that to this angry, indifferent stranger.

He was raising the tent with swift, experienced hands. Miranda watched the play of muscles under his jacket as he hauled up the complicated folds with the ease of a man folding a tablecloth.

She thought suddenly, He must be very strong. And she found she didn't want to think about how strong he might be.

'So your father wanted his son with him. To carry on his work?' The mockery was still there.

Miranda said stiffly, 'I taught reading and writing. Geography to the older children. A bit of botany.'

He was frowning. 'And I never heard of you. He did an amazing job at keeping you quiet. I wouldn't have believed it possible.'

Miranda lifted her chin. 'For that matter I've never heard him speak of a Paul.'

All this won her was an amused flicker at the corner of his mouth.

'He probably thought I wasn't a fit subject for children,' he said. 'Steal my map, yes; let the devil's name pass his lips, no.' He didn't sound concerned.

Miranda frowned. A curl of memory stirred. 'Your map?' she said slowly.

He shrugged. 'I drew it. Harry decided he needed it more than I did. It's not important. Come on. Climb into the tent. At least we can dry out.'

Miranda tried to stand up and thought better of it. Instead she half crawled, half wriggled across to the tent flap. Paul watched her frowningly. But he didn't say anything until she was inside.

'Take everything off until you get down to clothes that are dry,' he instructed. 'I'm going to see to Lemanja.' He straightened and then put his head back inside the flap. 'And dry that cat.'

He flung a rough cloth in after her. In the darkness of his departure she found that it was thin and worn but as dry as a bone. Miranda stripped off her jacket and trousers and began to rub hard at her damp skin. The trousers were soaked below the knee but the jacket had kept the worst of the rain off.

She could see the bright glow of the flashlight through the side of the tent. He was moving about purposefully. She heard him swear once. Once she heard the mare snorting and stamp a little. Immediately the shadow figure on the tent wall rose from its half crouch and disappeared. Miranda heard him talking soothingly to the horse.

More soothingly than he'd spoken to her, Miranda thought wryly. The man clearly hadn't much time for people unlearned in the ways of the wild. Or maybe he just didn't like taking responsibility for someone like that. In her heart of hearts, she thought, sighing, she really couldn't blame him for that.

The tent flap opened again and he thrust her pack inside. It had been opened. At once all Miranda's tolerance evaporated.

Paul was sublimely unaware of it. 'Not a bad load,' he told her. 'You've obviously learned something after all.'

The indifferently voiced compliment brought Miranda's blood to somewhere near boiling point.

'Thank you,' she said between her teeth.

But he was turning away.

'A fire's going to be difficult.'

'Make that impossible,' Miranda muttered. She didn't see that, after that drenching, any of the sticks with which the forest floor was plentifully provided would be dry enough to catch. 'But if Superman doesn't see that, then he'll stay outside long enough for me to get into dry trousers. Which,' she told the kitten, 'is all to the good.'

She managed to scramble into the desired garments before he returned, confounding her expectations about the fire. When he reappeared with a tin plate of hot minced stuff, Miranda didn't know whether to be delighted or annoyed. In the end, greed won. But it was a close-run thing, she acknowledged to herself wryly.

He brought the flashlight into the tent and adjusted the fierce beam by a series of complicated shutters. Then he settled down opposite her, cross-legged, and began to eat his own meal.

Miranda shifted uncomfortably. It was plain that the tent was only designed to hold one person. The enforced proximity made her heart beat suffocatingly. She hadn't been this close to a stranger since she was a child. The fact that he appeared completely unmoved by it didn't make it any easier to bear.

Paul sent her a shrewd look over his plate.

'You're very nervous for an intrepid missionary.'

'I'm not a missionary.'

His brows rose as if he didn't quite believe her. 'No? And what does Harry have to say about that?'

A very great deal and most of it angry. Even angrier now that he was beginning to realise that she had a will of her own and was intending to take charge of her own life. But Miranda wasn't telling a stranger that, either. She shrugged.

Paul put his plate down and linked his arms round one knee, watching her. In spite of the relaxed pose, Miranda felt as if she was under a microscope. She tensed.

'What's your name?' he demanded.

Miranda jumped. She should have prepared herself for that one, she thought, vexed. It would be patently obvious that she hadn't. And that she didn't intend to tell him the truth. There was a half-second's pause that sounded like an accusation.

'Mark,' she said defiantly, knowing it was too late.

One eyebrow went up.

'I take it the mission centre in São Paulo don't know about you either?'

She shook her head.

'Now, why?' he mused—almost, Miranda thought resentfully, as if he wasn't talking to her but himself. He sounded intrigued and—she realised it with slow-burning wrath—amused. As if she had been transported to the Brazilian jungle to provide him with a briefly entertaining puzzle. 'Aren't missionaries supposed to have their children with them? Does it distract them from the work in hand? Divert their love from its proper object?'

'I don't know what you're talking about,' she snapped.

He gave her a lop-sided smile, unmoved by the flare of temper. 'In the Middle Ages nuns weren't allowed to have pet dogs in case they loved the animals more than their Saviour.'

Miranda stared. 'I've never heard that before,' she said suspiciously.

The smile grew. 'I suppose you haven't. Wrong church, after all. But I assure you it's true. The point is, is it why Harry's been pretending you don't exist for five years?'

'No,' Miranda said positively.

There was no danger of Harry's attention being diverted, she thought. Most of the time he hardly noticed she was there. Or not unless he was trying to convince her of her vocation.

Paul's eyes narrowed. 'Then why?'

She did not like him but he had saved her life. She gave him a little bit more of the truth.

'My mother's family sent private detectives after me. Harry was afraid they'd persuade the Brazilian courts to send me back to England if they found me. Or, failing that, kidnap me.'

Her companion watched her in silence for an unnerving moment.

'And was that likely?'

Miranda bit her lip. It was a question she had often asked herself, particularly as she grew up.

'Harry said so.'

Another silence. The dark eyes were horribly keen, she discovered.

'And you wanted to stay?'

'Oh, *yes*.' There was no mistaking her fervour.

His eyes narrowed. 'Because you loved Harry? Or Brazil? Or because you were unhappy in England?'

'All three,' Miranda said a little breathlessly. She had the nastiest feeling that she was being interrogated by an expert.

He moved and she tensed. But all he was doing was feeling in his pack for a cheroot. He took out one of the long thin black cigarillos and lit it, narrowing his eyes at the curl of smoke. 'I know it's a disgusting habit,' he said, 'but I feel the occasion calls for it.' He swung round and stretched out his long legs, propping himself on one elbow. Miranda set her teeth. She could feel him watching her through the tobacco smoke.

'Did anyone ever try?' he asked lazily.

'Try what?'

'Extradition. Kidnap. Whatever.'

She looked down at her hands. 'People came looking, yes. Harry used to send me to the Indian village. João would come and tell me when they'd gone. I never met any of them.'

'João,' he said thoughtfully. It wasn't a question.

'Yes. Do you know him?'

Something in the way he was looking at her made her suddenly even more uneasy.

'No. Heitor does. He delivered their last child. It was Montes who sent us along to the mission this afternoon. Wild-goose chase, I thought. It never occurred to me that Harry would be so—careless.'

The words were drawled in a light, indifferent tone which would have raised Miranda's temper in other circumstances. As it was she had a horrid feeling that he was talking quite at random. And that whatever he was thinking about, behind the unreadable eyes and the languid voice, was not to her advantage.

She shifted, startling the kitten from its drowsy pose across her ankles. It began to explore the tent.

Paul's lashes swept down as he contemplated the little animal. They were the longest lashes Miranda had ever seen, fanning out on the tanned cheekbones like the fringe of a mask. She thought suddenly, Some women would find him irresistible.

The thought came from nowhere. Its force startled her. She said to herself wryly, What do I know about what women would find irresistible in men? Since Rolf went I've talked to no one—apart from the children—but Harry, João and Maria Clara who knows less about men than I do. And here I am assessing his sex appeal like a city teenager out of one of Maria Clara's comic books.

She shifted again, her expression constrained. She felt her cheeks burning and hoped that the uncertain light would hide it from Paul. Another thought occurred to her—more disturbing even than her reflections hitherto. If he knew she was a woman, would he, in his turn, have been wondering about her own attractions?

Maria Clara had a sister in Recife who sent her illustrated magazines full of highly coloured tales of uncontrollable passion. They hid them from Harry, of course, but the girls pored over each consignment, amused and wistful. The heroine was invariably pure and, above all, innocent, swept off her feet by a devilishly handsome man who was not either. Maria Clara and Miranda agreed that they could not imagine any of the men they knew behaving like these heroes. They agreed, regretfully, that it would not be comfortable if they did.

All of a sudden Miranda found that she could imagine a man behaving in that ruthless, piratical fashion without compunction or regret. She put a hand to her throat. Suddenly the atmosphere in the small tent was stifling.

His lashes lifted with startling suddenness. Miranda froze, like a rabbit trapped in a searchlight.

Paul said coolly, 'No need to look like that. I'm not going to lay a hand on you. If Harry were here I admit I'd be tempted to beat the hell out of him. But I don't take my feelings out on scapegoats. I think you'd better tell me what Harry's been up to.'

Miranda stared at him, genuinely bewildered. 'Harry? Been up to? You talk as if he's a criminal,' she said indignantly.

The man's mouth slanted upwards. It was a cynical smile and quite without humour. It sent an odd little shiver through her.

'No, I don't think he's a criminal,' he said in an even tone. 'I think he's an obsessed bigot without compassion or charity.' His voice was like ice. 'He seems to think he can do any damned thing he pleases as long as he can claim it's for the glory of God. God as interpreted by Henry Lane, of course, as sole possessor of the exclusive rights.'

Miranda flinched. In spite of the level tone, she sensed real anger licking through it. Harry would have been outraged by the accusation. He would have treated the man to one of his famous diatribes, she had no doubt. But Miranda felt confused and even a little afraid. She had, she realised, stumbled on a long-standing antagonism.

Had Harry shared it? If so, why hadn't he mentioned the man? Harry was not secretive, especially not about his battles with his enemies. Her presence at the mission was the only secret she had ever known Harry to keep and that was more for her benefit than his, as he often reminded her.

So who was this man? She searched her memory. She drew a blank.

She was distracted by the kitten, which began to sniff the scuffed toes of Paul's boots. They were covered in mud but nothing could disguise their expensive cut and even more expensive soft leather. Miranda was almost wholly inexperienced in the cost of clothes but she knew about good boots, if only because the mission was never able to afford them.

So he was rich.

She said abruptly, 'Who are you?'

His mouth twitched as if she amused him. But he answered her gravely enough.

'Paul Branco.'

'Branco?' Miranda frowned. There was something familiar about the name. She racked her brains but it eluded her.

She tried for a clue. 'How do you know Harry?'

The look he sent her was incredulous. 'In this territory it's virtually impossible not to know every European for a hundred square miles. Except you, of course. Which brings us back to my question.' He held out his fingers to the kitten who sniffed them with interest. He said casually, 'What does Harry think he is going to do with you?'

Miranda sighed. 'Train me,' she said at last.

The long lashes flicked up in undisguised astonishment.

'To take over from him? You're not serious.'

She grimaced. 'There's been a fall off in recruits to the ministry. Harry thinks he can keep it in the family, as it were.'

The little cat decided he was safe. It began to climb confidently up the muscular leg. Paul made no move to brush it away. Indeed he seemed hardly to notice it. He was frowning.

'Are you happy with that?' he asked slowly.

No, was the answer. No, and getting unhappier by the day as she and Harry fought over it in the noisy shouting matches followed by days of hurt silence with which her father punished her. But she knew that she had no vocation. More, she knew that Harry did not need her. She had gambled that he did when she decided to come out to Brazil. Now that it was obvious that Harry needed no one but himself, there was nothing left for her here.

She had to leave. She knew it. Maria Clara and João knew it. The only person she still had to convince was Harry. And she was working on that. But she was not going to say any of that to this arrogant, contemptuous stranger.

So Miranda bent her head and mumbled an incomprehensible answer through a mouthful of spicy beans. Her companion looked briefly amused. He gave an impatient sigh.

'How can you tell, a child of your age? What do the mission headquarters say?'

Miranda was by no means sure that Harry had told them. She mumbled again. The kitten had progressed to Paul Branco's arm and was snuffling in the crook of his elbow. He stroked the little head absently.

'The man ought to be locked up,' he said in evident exasperation. 'What in hell's name was he doing, leaving you alone in that mission with a hurricane warning out?'

Miranda could answer that one without venturing on to treacherous ground. 'He said we had to have faith,' she reported.

Her companion snorted. 'That sounds like Harry. It was pure chance that Heitor bumped into Montes, you realise? We might never have come anywhere near the place.'

Miranda shivered. 'I know,' she said quietly.

'Of course, you were getting ready to leave, weren't you?' The impatient expression softened for a moment. 'Were you afraid?'

'Terrified,' Miranda said frankly.

He laughed. 'You're a brave kid, aren't you?' He looked down at the kitten, now resting on his arm with its paws folded under it and its eyes closed in ecstasy under his caressing finger. His look of amusement deepened. 'Of course, you had your lion for protection.'

She gave a shaken laugh. 'I was glad of the company, to be honest. You must think that's awfully feeble.'

He sent her a curious underbrowed look. 'No. I think it's very—human.'

She had the feeling he had been intending to say something else and had stopped himself at the last moment. He was watching her frowningly.

'So Harry's been training you up to take over the family business and you don't want to.' His voice was dry. 'What's he going to say when he finds out that his secret is out?'

That had been beginning to exercise Miranda's mind too. Harry would be furious with her. She did not look forward to it with any enthusiasm at all. But she was not going to admit that to a stranger either. So she shrugged.

'It can't be helped. He'll have to see that.'

He raised his eyebrows. 'Will he?' he murmured.

'I shall point out that I had faith, as he said. And the Lord provided you to come and rescue me,' she said fluently.

Paul Branco gave a shout of laughter. Miranda gave him a shy smile, pleased. He sobered.

'Fair enough. I have no quarrel with that and I doubt if the Lord would have either. Harry, however, is another matter. Harry doesn't approve of me.'

Miranda gave him a dry look. 'That seems to be mutual.'

This time his eyebrows flew up as if she had surprised him.

'You're right, of course,' he said after a pause. 'We—disagreed some years ago.'

Miranda's heart sank. Harry disagreed with everyone except the tolerant Indians who placidly accepted everything he said and then went their own way. She had learned to model her own behaviour on that of the Indians. She sometimes thought that with his fellow Europeans Harry was at permanent war.

'What did you fight about?'

His mouth slanted. 'Morals and land rights. To be more specific, my morals and the Indians' land rights.' The memory amused him. 'Harry thought he had a God-given duty to rewrite both. I—er—dissuaded him.'

Memory shifted. She could almost hear Harry saying something. What was it? Something about seduction? And someone he called a wicked man. Could that have been that Paul Branco?

'No one ever dissuades Harry,' she said absently.

'Well, I did,' Paul Branco said calmly. 'He wanted to build a mission centre in the middle of tribal lands. I stopped it.'

Miranda shook her head. 'He must have been furious,' she said, impressed. If only she had paid more attention when Harry was talking. 'Why have I never heard of you?' she murmured.

'I don't think Harry is the sort of man who talks too much about his failures,' her companion replied drily.

Miranda sighed. 'No, that's true.' She grimaced. 'Gosh, he's going to be angry when he hears it was you who pulled me out of the mission building.'

He grinned. It was a carefree grin, almost reckless. It gave him a rakish charm which made Miranda blink. She had been seeing him wholly in terms of slightly impatient commands. The charm was a shock.

'You are so right. And for more reasons than I am currently prepared to discuss,' he said with an irony which Miranda did not understand.

He saw her expression of confusion. He gave a soft laugh.

'When he stole the map I drew, he left me a note. It was years ago, during the battle of the mission site. He said that he was removing it so that good should come forth out of evil.'

Miranda's memory stirred again, uncomfortably. 'He said it was the work of the devil,' she said slowly.

'Well, it was my work. Which must make me the devil, wouldn't you say?'

CHAPTER THREE

MIRANDA jumped. There was an odd resonance to it.

She was not afraid of Paul Branco, she told herself. Of course she was not afraid of him. She might not like him. He had a regrettable tendency to order her around. But he had been just as imperious with nice Heitor. It was not a characteristic that was reserved for his dealing with her. He had been kind enough, if impatient. After five years of living on the edge of the rainforest, after five years with Harry she had learned that there were more things worth being afraid of than a caustic tongue.

So of course she was not afraid of him. Yet his calmly announcing that he must be the devil sent a *frisson* of unease up her spine.

Miranda said sharply, 'That's not funny.'

His reply was cool. 'Oh, but it is. You have no idea.'

She might not be afraid of him but she was rapidly developing a healthy dislike of this confident man who amused himself by laughing at her.

'Then explain it,' she challenged.

He lifted his shoulders. 'You would need to know a lot more about me—and the world—to appreciate it.'

Smug, condescending, arrogant man. Dislike was almost too mild a word for what she could feel for him, Miranda discovered. But five years had taught her diplomacy as well.

'Then I shall hope to learn both in time,' she said with deceptive meekness.

It was a tone that usually worked on Harry. It was one she often used to deflect her father. To her considerable annoyance it had less success with Paul Branco.

His eyebrows went up and he looked, if anything, even more amused.

'That could be uncomfortable,' he murmured, making no attempt to disguise that private laughter. 'For both of us.'

Her meek demeanour faltered. He laughed aloud.

'No, you don't understand that either and I'm not going to enlighten you,' he said kindly but with great firmness. 'I know you think it's very unfair, my child. I can even sympathise. But, believe me, we'll be much better off not exchanging views on each other's character until we get to the safety of my house. Where,' he added ironically, 'there will be other people to referee.'

Miranda hunched a shoulder. 'I wish you wouldn't keep calling me a child.'

Paul Branco's mouth twitched. 'It's a useful reminder to both of us.'

She stared. 'A reminder? Of what?'

'That things aren't always what they seem.' He was bland.

'You mean you seem like the devil but you're an angel really?' Miranda enquired sweetly. 'Or the reverse?'

He gave another of those shouts of laughter.

'Tomorrow,' he said. 'When there's someone else to see fair play. Finish your beans. We need to get some sleep.'

He finished his own meal rapidly. Then he sat back, propping himself against his bedroll. The small cat was still purring sleepily on his arm. He looked down at it, amused.

'Not much upsets his equilibrium, does it?' he said, tickling the top if its head between the ears. 'He never stirred during the ride. Or I didn't detect it, anyway.'

You didn't detect I was not a boy, Miranda thought. It was a small private amusement of her own. She needed it.

She forked up the last of the beans. 'They sleep a lot at that age.'

'Even when they're being bounced up and down?'

She said wryly, 'We didn't bounce that much. Scramble more like. The kitten wouldn't have felt it. As far as he was concerned he was warm and dry and that was enough.'

'Not a bad philosophy for the rainforest,' Paul Branco observed.

'I suppose not.' Miranda was shaken by a little laugh. 'It was all I was aiming for when you found me after all.'

The harsh face softened briefly. 'That was brave.'

'No, it wasn't,' Miranda said positively. 'I was scared out of my wits.'

'That's what makes it brave.'

He picked the little cat up gently and settled it in the corner, impervious to its sleepy protests. He began to unroll the bedsheet with efficient, controlled movements. Miranda drew up her legs to be out of his way. It was hardly necessary, she found. Amazingly he managed to have the thing neatly in position without encroaching on her space at all.

When he had finished he knelt at the end of the sheet, one elbow on his bent knee, and regarded her thoughtfully.

'I wasn't planning on company,' he said. 'We'll have to do the best we can.'

Miranda was doubtful. There was no question of either of them sleeping outside the tent. Water was still dripping audibly and steadily on to the canvas.

'What do you suggest?'

'We'll have to share,' he said coolly. 'It reduces the layers between us and the ground but it can't be helped. It's only for one night, please God.' He pointed a long finger at the edge of the waterproof sheet by the tent wall. 'You lie down here. Then I'll get in beside you and pull the sheet over both of us. That way I can get out to see to Lemanja if there is lightning.'

Miranda looked at the narrow sheet and swallowed hard. As he had said, it was designed for one person.

She would inevitably be crushed up against that arrogant, powerful body through the hours of darkness.

Paul Branco said softly, 'And it's not a suggestion.' She searched his face. All softness had left it now. He looked tough, competent and very determined. 'It's an order.'

She gave in.

It was not the most comfortable night of her life.

Paul Branco, she found, slept with unnatural stillness. In fact for two pins, as she lay looking at the dark bar of his shoulders which formed her horizon, she would have accused him of not sleeping at all. Miranda herself was finding sleep almost impossible.

Not that Paul Branco had made it difficult. In fact getting herself stretched out on the makeshift bed had been accomplished with a lack of embarrassed revelations that Miranda would not have dared to hope for. He had left her to get into the sheet on her own while he saw to the horse and rinsed their plates in the continuing rain.

At once she had seized the opportunity of privacy. She'd pulled the concealing hat down hard over her hair and secured it with the hairpins she had used to pin up her plaits on the top of her head. She'd skewered it on so tight that her eyes had watered with pain.

When he'd returned she'd had the green sheet clutched to her chin. Her boots had stood upright against her backpack. He'd looked at them ruefully.

'I'm grateful,' he told her. 'I wasn't looking forward to being kicked by those boots. You may have difficulty getting into them tomorrow, though.'

Miranda was suddenly supremely grateful that she had managed to disguise her sex from him.

She said in a voice that strove for normality, 'I don't kick.'

Paul Branco was amused. 'You'd better not. You'll have the whole tent down.'

She managed a laugh but the picture he conjured up was not comfortable. Nor were the stories she was remembering all too vividly from Maria Clara's magazines. For the first time she thought perhaps Harry had been right when he'd condemned them.

Harry said they undermined the reader's moral fibre. Miranda had always thought they were innocent entertainment and continued to read them without Harry's knowledge. Now, alone for the first time in her life with a man that even her limited experience recognised as devastating, she wondered. Without those romantic dramas in her memory, would she be watching her rescuer's every move with trembling self-consciousness?

It was all in her imagination, she told herself firmly. Paul Branco was certainly not aware of her, except as an annoying youth for whom he was temporarily responsible. As long as he remained in ignorance, she would be fine.

Just for a moment Miranda wondered what he would do if he knew she was a girl. The hero of *Night of Passion* had no sooner had the lovely Xanthe in his power than he had overwhelmed her with his passion. Looking at Paul Branco's cool, amused expression, Miranda realised that she could not imagine him overwhelmed by anything, certainly not uncontrollable passion for a skinny girl only just out of adolescence whom he didn't even like.

As for herself—well, she had already established that she was not afraid of him. Just because she could detect the play of powerful muscles under his bush shirt in the harsh lantern light, that was no reason to lose her head. Or her self-possession.

He looked down at her then. Miranda thought his mouth thinned. But she could not be quite sure in the heavy shadows cast by the lantern. Unexpectedly he leaned forward and doused it in a movement that might almost have been angry.

He sat down with his back to her and hauled off his own boots rather more expeditiously than she had.

Miranda cleared her throat.

'Do you do a lot of this?'

'What?' He did not turn but his dark head cocked to indicate that he was listening.

'Camping.'

'It's not my preferred recreation,' he said ironically. 'Especially not in a force nine gale with a flood warning out.'

'But you know what you're doing.'

'Of course.' He sounded faintly surprised. 'I've done my time under canvas. No one who lives on the edge of the rainforest should be without the knowledge to survive in the open if he has to.'

He turned and took hold of the corner of the sheet. He slid down on to his back, taking the sheet neatly over both of them.

Miranda cleared her throat.

'This is my first time.'

There was a little pause. Then he said with unwarranted dryness, 'That is obvious.'

She felt hurt. 'I'm sorry. I'm doing my best.'

He gave a sharp little sigh. 'I'm sure you are. Go to sleep.'

But she wanted his approval, it seemed. To her own annoyance, Miranda heard herself say humbly, 'I'll do whatever you want. I don't want to be a burden.'

This time the pause was longer. And oddly charged.

He shifted; she tensed—but he was only freeing his left arm to put it under his head as he stared at the tent roof.

'This,' he remarked, 'is a first for me too, I have to confess.' He sounded strained. In spite of that there was still the amusement that she had come to expect licking through the deep voice. 'I—don't want you to do anything, my child. Except go to sleep.'

There was finality in his tones. Miranda knew he was right. She was going to be tired in the morning as it was. And God knew how far they had to travel on that poor burdened horse the next day.

But even though she knew he was right, even though she closed her eyes and willed herself to rest, she found it was impossible to sleep properly. She was too conscious of the surprising warmth of his body.

She heard his steady breathing. She inhaled the herbal scent of whatever he washed his hair in. And every time she moved she brushed against him in an intimacy she had never shared with anyone in her life.

In spite of her brave resolutions, it was alarming. And it did not make for a peaceful night.

In the morning she was heavy-eyed. By contrast, Paul Branco looked alert and in control.

'The wind's down,' he told her as she stirred.

Miranda made a business of coming awake. In practice she was certain she had been lying there wakeful, listening to the noises of the forest, as long as he had. She rubbed her eyes with finger and thumb. They felt gritty from lack of sleep.

'Rain?' she asked.

He sat up and unwound the sheet from round his legs.

'Doesn't sound like it.' He looked at her briefly. 'Can you deal with the bedroll?'

Miranda was not at all sure. Certainly she did not have his unflappable expertise. But she was not going to admit defeat until she had tried.

'I'll have a go,' she said crisply.

He rolled off the bed and went in a crouch to the tent flap.

'Do that. I'll see if I can find us some breakfast.'

As soon as he was gone Miranda shot upright. Her hat had lurched over her eye at a drunken angle. Soft brown tendrils were escaping along her neck and above the revealed ear. She straightened it hastily.

At least Branco had been too preoccupied to notice that, she congratulated herself. Of course, there was no reason why a young man should not have hair to his shoulder-blades. He was not likely to put it up in two schoolgirl plaits, though. Her hair would almost certainly have given away her sex.

Of course, Paul Branco would have to know that she was a girl eventually. She was not a fool and she had recognised that somewhere in the middle of the night, listening to his even breathing. It had made her heart lurch uncomfortably. Of course she would tell him, she told herself stoutly. She just did not want to confront him with the knowledge after they had spent a trying night together. Or while they were still alone.

She tucked her shirt more firmly into the waistband of her trousers and puffed up the concealing folds of her jacket. Then she dealt with the sheet as well as she could.

She was not helped by the kitten. Wakeful now, he clearly decided that the unmaking of last night's bed was a game especially designed for his entertainment. He rolled in its folds, turned over on his back with all four sets of claws extruding through the material and mewed imperatively.

Laughing, Miranda scooped him out of his tangle and hoisted him on to her shoulder. There he made little darts at escaping curls while she folded the thing along its previous creases as well as she could.

Paul Branco, pushing back the flap to come back into the tent, stopped dead at the sight. Miranda looked up, laughing. The kitten was trying to pat her eyelashes and she was shaking her head to avoid him. Something in Paul Branco's still face, though, made her amusement die at once. In its place came something much deeper and more complicated. It made her hold her breath, as if she were waiting for the end of the world.

He moved into the tent, stooping. His hand came out. Miranda's eyes widened. She stood very still, as if she had seen a spider whose poisonous qualities she was not sure about. His hand brushed her cheek. She drew in a breath that rasped in the silence between them like a scream.

She waited for one of his acid comments. But he said nothing. He was only plucking the cat off her shoulder. He turned and put it down gently just outside the tent.

'I hope you like sour-sop,' he said, turning back to her. His voice sounded strained. Or was that her overheated imagination? 'That's all I can find for breakfast.'

He held out the big fruit. Miranda expelled a rather shaky breath. Restored to normality, she made a face. She did not like the taste of sour-sop though the local people regarded it as a delicacy. The fruit was also singularly ugly. It looked like an enormous avocado pear covered with spines.

'They look like bad-tempered pineapples,' she said, receiving it gingerly.

It was a heavy specimen, probably five pounds or so. She took both hands to it. He crossed the tent and produced a knife with a carved wooden handle and a wickedly practical eighteen-inch blade.

'They're no beauties, I agree. But it will give us energy for the ride. It's going to be filthy,' he said brutally. 'Some of the paths have been washed away. All the rocks are soaked and treacherous. Give the thing here.'

He took the fruit back and the knife sliced into it as if its tough hide were made of butter. Warm butter, Miranda thought as the fruit fell into triangular pieces under his efficient ministrations. She took a piece, eyeing the knife warily.

'That looks lethal.'

He looked down it. 'This?' he said affectionately. He tossed it quickly into a perfect circle and caught it one-handed. 'No point in having a knife if it doesn't cut.'

'I'm surprised you didn't bring your machete.'

'I did.'

Miranda was taken aback. Paul glinted a smile down at her.

'I don't know what damage the storm will have done. I came prepared. I can get us through anything but fallen trees. And I can get us over those.'

Miranda swallowed. She was beginning to realise just what a risk she would have been taking in going into the forest on her own. She said so.

He shrugged. 'You'd have been all right. You're obviously level-headed. It would just have taken you a bit longer to get anywhere.' He speared a piece of sour-sop and waved it at her. 'Eat.'

Miranda grimaced and put the piece she was holding against her mouth. As usual the fruit had the texture of slightly scented cotton wool. But she knew Paul was right. It was very sweet and they would need that sugar for energy on the next leg of their journey. Avoiding a large brown seed, she took a mouthful of the white stuff and chewed.

He watched her for a moment. His lips twitched. He had a beautifully sculpted mouth, Miranda thought.

'Don't swallow it, if you hate it,' he advised. 'Just suck the juice.'

Miranda was relieved. She carefully removed the fibrous stuff she had been working round and round her mouth.

'Eventually I start to gag,' she said apologetically.

He shrugged. 'Cordon bleu it isn't. But it has its uses. We'll take the rest with us. We're getting low on water. I collected some last night but it's not enough to fill the water bottles.'

Miranda was surprised. 'But—the river?'

'The river,' he said patiently, 'will be pure mud by this time. Even with purification tablets, you wouldn't want to drink it.'

She bit her lip. 'I'm a real liability, aren't I?'

He looked across at her. There was an enigmatic expression in his eyes.

'I wouldn't say that,' he drawled. 'A complication, rather. But you can't help that. Anyway, it will soon be over. I aim to reach the *fazenda* by tonight.'

They did. It was not an easy journey. The wind had fallen, leaving with it a devastation of fallen trees and uprooted bushes. The rain held off but there was a steady drip of accumulated water falling off the high leaves above their heads. Most of the time Miranda could not see the sky. Walking in the jungle floor felt like being in a huge, wild cathedral, she thought, where at any moment some celestial organ might break into music and shatter mere mortals to pieces with the sound.

Paul was undismayed by the vastness, or by the destruction, it seemed. He took them steadily up hill. They spent more time walking, Paul leading the patient Lemanja, than they did on the horse's back. They wound round and round, she thought sometimes in nearly complete circles. The trees were immensely tall, as if when they were still warm a giant hand had reached down and stretched them up and up to the sky.

There were huge lianas suspended from some of them. Paul snapped one off and cut it swiftly down to make a hiker's stick to help Miranda. She was surprised to feel how strong and rigid it was. Against the trees the lianas looked as frail as string.

Sometimes the forest floor was almost clear, covered with last year's leaves and bracken. Sometimes it was so densely wooded that Paul had to use the machete to hack a way for them. At least twice they had to climb among the roots as if on castle ramparts, Paul coaxing the horse with gentle encouragement. Below them the river surged audibly.

It was wild and dangerous, Miranda knew. But it was exhilarating too. She saw lots of firecrackers, the cluster of red tubular flowers along the stem producing the effect of a scarlet finger pointing accusingly at the trees that were shutting out its light. And once, in the afternoon when the forest was so still she thought nothing was moving but themselves, she saw a humming bird. It was a little below them, further down the slope of the valley. Its wings were fizzing. It was a tremulous blur of rainbow colours as the black length of its beak hooked into a firecracker flower.

She gave an exclamation of delight and stopped. Paul followed her pointing finger. Briefly, his expression relaxed.

'Beautiful,' he said. 'You'll see more of them at the *fazenda*. Come on.'

But Miranda was entranced by the tiny bird, shimmering like a jewel among the green shadows. 'It's so— alive,' she said, awed.

For a moment he stopped too. He scanned her expression of wonder. Briefly his face softened.

'Raw, unbridled life. The rainforest's speciality,' he said drily. Briefly, she thought his hand touched her cheek. 'If you want to stay alive too, you'd better move, though.'

Reluctantly, looking back, she moved.

'Watch where you're putting your feet,' he reminded her.

He was driving them at a cracking pace. He let her have breaks to drink and suck a triangle of sour-sop but each one was no more than five minutes. Eventually, she began to droop and even the horse seemed to stumble more often. But Paul was tireless.

She missed her footing on a clump of mud that she had taken for a rock. It dissolved under her. She called out, more in surprise than hurt.

In a second Paul had caught her up, one arm round her waist, clamping her to his side. Miranda felt as if all the breath had been knocked out of her. As if, instead of saving her from harm, he was the one who had pushed her into danger.

He looked at her closely before setting her back on her feet with care. 'Pity to break an ankle so close to home,' he drawled after a moment.

'Home?' She hardly dared to ask.

He nodded at the curtain of trees ahead of them. 'Can't you see the path?'

Miranda looked hopefully but she saw nothing. They went on, Paul striding ahead. Then suddenly the slope became less precipitous. All of a sudden she could see a path. The tiredness fell from her. She quickened her pace.

They came out into a clearing. She could hear water.

'Waterfall,' Paul said, nodding briefly in the direction of the sound. 'We're now on Branco land.' He glanced down at her. 'Bearing up?'

'Bearing up,' Miranda nodded.

Now that rest and a roof over her head were close, she gave him a brilliant smile. Paul blinked.

'You ride Lemanja,' he said. 'I'll lead. There may be some fallen trees on the path.'

Without waiting for her agreement he picked her up and hoisted her into the saddle. Lemanja stood steadily enough but the mare tossed her head and snorted a little at this unworthy burden. The kitten, back in Miranda's jacket, mewed in reproach. Miranda patted the horse's neck, laughing.

She looked down, inviting him to share her amusement. She found that Paul was looking up at her with a very strange expression on his face. Miranda's laughter died.

'I'm sorry. Am I wasting time?' she said nervously to that frowning expression.

He seemed to shake himself. 'No. It was me,' he said politely. 'We must hurry if we are to get there before dark.'

They did not quite manage that. But his multi-faceted lantern could be adjusted to provide a strong forward beam. He hooked it on to his belt and they accomplished the last half-hour of the journey in its swinging light.

Miranda was swaying in the saddle herself by the time she realised that they were approaching a house. She heard the voices first. Then they rounded a corner and she saw a two-storey colonial house, ablaze with lights.

'It looks like paradise,' she said.

So indeed it proved. Paul took the horse direct to the stables where his arrival was greeted with restrained elation.

'Heitor radioed,' a tall moustached man said, taking Lemanja's bridle. 'This the boy from Lane's?'

Paul lifted her lightly out of the saddle and set her on her feet. He turned her gently into the light from the stable. The moustached man's face was impassive but Miranda got the impression that he was considerably startled.

'What's the damage like?' Paul asked.

The other shrugged, his eyes lingering on her before he turned to answer. 'Too soon to tell. Roofs aren't good, though.' He led Lemanja off in the direction of a stall. Then he paused. 'Bebel Martins brought in the German woman,' he added as an afterthought.

Paul looked down at Miranda. She thought she detected a gleam of relief in his eyes. She wondered at it.

But all he said was, 'Two missionaries under a leaking roof. There's got to be a moral in there somewhere.'

Miranda realised who the German woman had to be. 'You mean Lotte Meyer is here?' she asked doubtfully.

Lotte was a colleague of Harry's. That meant that Miranda was always banished when Lotte paid her annual visit. She was also the person who was supposed to be accompanying him into the jungle on the crusade for new converts. Miranda bit her lip.

Paul flicked an eyebrow up. 'Kept you of sight of Fräulein Meyer too, did he?' he said drily. 'Too late to do anything about it now. This is an emergency.'

He put a hand under her elbow and took her through a covered walkway.

After the forest it was like the paradise she had called it. Wall-mounted lamps shed a warm golden glow over old stone and springy grass. Here and there the deep shadows of climbing plants, so unlike the black, suffocating wildness of the rainforest, wavered in the rising wind. There was a wonderful smell of rain-soaked blossom.

As Miranda followed Paul's long stride, the honey scent of the trumpet-shaped blooms was replaced by something altogether homelier: coffee and warm bread and distant friendly buzz. She drew a little grateful breath.

'Magic,' she said softly. She had not had such a sense of peace and comfort for years. If ever, she thought wryly. 'You're right. We're home.' She staggered a little.

Paul looked down at her then. He was wearing a curious expression. 'You're out on your feet. What you need is a bowl of soup and then bed.'

He pushed open a big wooden door at the end of the covered walkway. It led into a kitchen. At least that was what Miranda deduced it was; she had never seen such a room in her life.

It was full of light and warmth. And people. The noise, after the watery solemnity of the forest, was indescribable. Miranda almost staggered under it. Paul did not let go of her elbow. Instead he called out in a bellow that shook her eardrums, 'Anna.'

There was an eddy in the crowd and a large lady appeared out of it.

'Oh, you're back,' she said without noticeable excitement. 'Heitor wants you to radio as soon as you can.'

Paul nodded. 'Fine. Only give this scrap a meal while I do so, will you?'

Anna looked at Miranda narrow-eyed. The kitten, sensing warmth, was wriggling out of her jacket. Anna caught the small animal with no more surprise than she had shown at Paul's arrival and grinned cheerfully. 'Two meals,' she said.

Paul chuckled and released Miranda's elbow.

Anna sat her down on a bench at a long table and put a plate of stew in front of her along with a large glass of water. The kitten, as far as Miranda could see, got the same stew.

She ate hungrily but before she was halfway through she could feel her head begin to nod. Paul came back, threading his way round makeshift tables. Miranda watched him. He had a word for a lot of the people assembled there against the storm.

As he was passing one table, a tall woman stood up and put her hand on his arm. He turned, an expression of delighted surprise on his face.

'Bebel. You're still here.'

His arm went round her. For some reason Miranda averted her eyes. Suddenly she was not hungry.

'And who are you?' The voice belonged to a small grey-haired woman with horn-rimmed glasses. She did not sound very approving, Miranda thought.

'I was at the mission,' she said carefully.

'At the mission?' It was sharp. 'At Henry Lane's mission? How could you have been at the mission?'

'Leave the inquisition till tomorrow, Fräulein Meyer, hmm?' drawled a husky voice. 'The child needs to sleep.'

Miranda swung round, relieved. Paul looked down at her and flicked her cheek with long fingers.

'No explanations tonight.'

The woman, who had to be Lotte Meyer, looked dissatisfied. As well she might, thought Miranda. But Paul was right: she was just not up to parrying the other woman's questions tonight. She became aware that she was bone-weary.

'A bed sounds wonderful,' she said truthfully.

'Come with me, then.'

She stood up. Then she stopped, looking round.

'What is it?' Paul was impatient.

'The cat. My cat. I can't abandon him. Not after we've come so far together.'

He made a rude noise, half-laughter half-scorn. He spied the cat under the table and scooped it up, depositing it in her arms.

'There you are. And if he cries in the night he's your responsibility.'

He towed her through the crowd and ushered her through a door into a panelled hallway.

'He didn't last night.'

He glanced down at her. 'Last night he knew what was good for him. If he'd opened his mouth I'd have killed him,' he said coolly. 'Last night was inordinately trying in a number of ways. I am still trying to forget last night.'

'I know,' said Miranda, sighing.

His eyebrows went up at that. But he said nothing, leading the way up a magnificent curving staircase. At another time the richness would have awed Miranda. But now she was too tired to notice.

Paul took her along a corridor that echoed to the swift pace of his heels on the polished floor. She noticed tapestries that must surely be old, and precious and superb carvings. But she was too tired to comment.

When I'm awake, Miranda thought wryly, I'm going to feel seriously out of place. She stumbled after him. Thank God I'm not awake, she added to herself.

Paul flung open a door. The room beyond was high-ceilinged, panelled and furnished with the richness of an earlier century. Clutching the cat to her, Miranda blinked. She went in slowly.

Paul stood in the doorway.

'There's a shirt in the chest you can use to sleep in. If you want a shower——' his voice suggested that it was not very likely '—the bathroom is through there.'

'Thank you,' said Miranda.

She put the cat down and sat on the edge of the brocade-covered bed. An indefinable perfume hung about the rich hangings, as if hundreds of elegant women had occupied it before her. She felt horribly young and uncertain. And dirty.

She said wistfully, thinking of the kitchen full of waifs, 'I suppose I couldn't have a bath?'

There was an odd little silence. Then Paul Branco laughed. For once it wasn't mocking. In fact he sounded rueful.

'If the hurricane does hit, the water supply will be a problem. But for the moment bath all you want. Just don't fall asleep and drown.'

He was gone.

Miranda found the bathroom was as dark with polished wood as the rest of the house. The bath was freestanding, a high Victorian affair on claw feet with enormous taps in the shape of mermaids. But the hot water was blessedly modern.

So was the store of bath oils and lotions on the marble-topped table. She had been right about her perfumed predecessors in this apartment, Miranda thought wryly.

She peeled off her filthy clothing with a sigh of pleasure and poured Elizabethan-rose-scented oil into the steaming water. She sank into it, up to her neck. Rotating her shoulders luxuriously, she gave a deep sigh of contentment.

All this luxury, she thought with the detachment of near exhaustion. I've never seen anything like it. Never even imagined it, still less in an isolated house in the middle of the jungle. And *he* seems to treat it all as if it were perfectly normal. She gave a little laugh, stretching in pure pleasure.

Harry will be horrified if he ever finds out I've been lolling about in the bath of the idle rich. Tomorrow, I'll think of my excuses. Tonight, I'll just soak here and... *He* said I wasn't to fall asleep, she reminded herself drowsily. I won't fall asleep. I'll just up the warm water a little more and...

The door to the bedroom banged back on its hinges.

'I thought so,' Paul Branco said grimly.

Miranda jumped, her heavy eyelids flying open in mingled guilt and shock. She tried to sink under the water, scarlet with embarrassment.

Paul Branco was not embarrassed but annoyed and impatient, and there was more than a hint of exasperation in the way he held out a huge fluffy towel to her. But he did not look at all embarrassed.

'Out. I warned you.'

'Go away.'

'My dear child, now we are home we can both stop pretending.'

Miranda snatched the towel and climbed out of the cooling water. She sent him a fulminating look. He met it drily and answered the silent question.

'My dear child, if you ride a horse in a man's arms for the best part of a day you must expect to be discovered,' he said.

'*Oh*!' It was like a shock of cold water. Her eyes fell away from his. 'You knew I wasn't a boy? Why didn't you *tell* me?' she cried in shocked distress.

'When should I have told you?' Paul Branco said, suddenly harsh. 'When we were sitting on top of each other in that tent and you were so scared, you almost stopped breathing? Or when we were cosily tucked up in the same bedsheet?'

Their eyes met. Miranda could not look away. Her eyes widened and widened, staring into the dark intensity of his. Was he *angry*? His mouth was tilted in a sardonic smile.

'No one else need know you ever pretended,' he said. 'And no one will talk—as long as you keep away from my quarters now you're here.'

Miranda tugged the towel tighter around her. She felt chilled all of a sudden. 'I don't understand.'

'Don't you, missionary's daughter?' His tone was jeering.

He crossed to her in three swift strides. His boots were loud on the polished boards. She stared up at him. He pulled her against him in a travesty of the gentle embrace in which she had seen him hold the tall woman downstairs. Although he was smiling, Miranda's impression that she had infuriated him somehow was even stronger.

'Then let me be more explicit. If you come anywhere near my room, you are risking—this.'

The kiss was ferocious. She felt as if she was being devoured. Maria Clara's magazines had not mentioned that the heroine might feel sheer shameful panic on these occasions.

Perhaps true heroines didn't, thought Miranda, her head swimming. Or perhaps real heroes behaved differently. Because she did not think that there was much chance that Paul Branco was in the throes of uncontrollable passion. Anger, yes, impatience, yes; passion, no.

But she had been right about one thing, Miranda thought dimly as his mouth ravaged hers and she clung to him in bewilderment. Somehow she had managed to make Paul Branco very angry indeed.

CHAPTER FOUR

MIRANDA pulled away from him, wide-eyed. She had a confused feeling, based on Maria Clara's magazines, that she should either have kissed him back or slapped his face. Instead she retreated two steps and drew the back of a rather shaky hand across her mouth.

His hands fell away. His eyes were glittering.

'W-why did you do that?' she said unsteadily.

'You should know the risks.'

'The—the risks?' She sounded like a stupid schoolgirl, Miranda thought in disgust. In all honesty she could not blame him for the cynical look of contempt with which he greeted her stammered question.

'One man, one woman.' He was ticking them off on mocking fingers. 'Darkness and danger.'

'But——'

'It's an explosive brew.'

She stared. 'I don't understand. You kissed me because of *that*? But we're safe now. We're not going to have to go back into the forest, I hope. And we're not alone any more. The house is full of people,' she said, thinking of the teeming kitchen.

'Now, yes. But we have been alone. Today and last night. In darkness and danger.' His voice was deliberate. 'In chemical terms, the fusion has already taken place. There's nothing I can do about that. Except try and contain it.'

Was he saying she had thrown herself at him last night? That she would take the opportunity of being in his house to do it again? How could he? She had done her level best not to touch him last night, to convince him that she was a boy, even.

'Aren't you looking round corners to find problems that don't exist?' Miranda's voice was cold.

'Where there's a young and beautiful woman there are always problems,' Paul said wryly. 'At least when I'm around, it seems.' He gave a sudden harsh laugh. 'Oh, God, and I don't even know your name.'

'Miranda,' she said absently.

She barely noticed that he had called her beautiful. For one thing she did not believe him. For another she was too angry at the insulting implication.

'You're at no risk from me,' she assured him, her spine arrow-straight.

He said softly, 'You think the risk is over, then?'

'I think the risk is all in your imagination,' she corrected him.

'Then you're even more naïve than I thought.'

The dismissive tone did nothing to sweeten her temper. Miranda's chin came up another couple of degrees. Her tiredness was forgotten in the white heat of indignation. But she did not shout and scream. Arguing with Harry had taught her that much, at least.

'Or you're more imaginative,' she pointed out sweetly.

An unpleasant gleam came into his eyes. 'Oh, I'm that all right,' he agreed.

He cancelled the space between them in one unhurried stride. Miranda refused to be intimidated. She did not give ground. Instead she tilted her chin even higher to look up into his face. She met his eyes levelly.

'So where does the risk lie? With you or me?'

He stared at her for an unnerving moment, his face perfectly blank. Then he shook his head. 'You really don't see, do you?' He sounded weary.

That was somehow the final insult. Her instinct was to blaze at him that she was not a lust-crazed teenager. But, with considerable self-control, Miranda curbed her instinct. She had a feeling that it would only serve to convince him that he was right about her naïveté.

'I don't see a problem, certainly. Other than in your own mind.'

'It's not my mind that's the problem,' Paul said with irony. 'Nor yours.'

'Then——?'

'Bodies, Miranda,' he interrupted almost savagely. 'Physical attraction. Chemical attraction. Whatever you call it. You can't see it but it's there.'

She began to feel alarmed. 'But we don't know each other.'

He closed his eyes briefly. 'We don't have to know each other. It was there the moment I touched you.'

She shook her head. 'But you thought I was a boy.'

'Did I?'

'Yes, you——' She broke off. She remembered the mockery in his voice when he had addressed her deliberately as 'boy', the way he had left her alone in the tent to undress. The way he had held her.

Her whole body flinched as if she had put a hand on a naked flame. Paul saw it. His expression gentled.

'If you'd lived anywhere but with that mad old man you'd have recognised it for yourself,' he said. 'Look, don't be afraid. I won't let you get hurt.'

Her head reared up again. 'I am not afraid,' Miranda said proudly.

The gentleness evaporated in sheer exasperation. 'Then you damned well should be. I am,' he told her brutally.

Miranda held on to her temper with an effort.

'You're in no danger from me.'

'Oh, yes, I am,' he said with irony. 'You don't know the half of it.'

Miranda put a hand to her head. 'Look, you're not making sense. I know I'm tired but you're talking as if we're people with no control over our own decisions...'

'Control?' Paul sounded incredulous. 'We're dancing on the edge of a volcano here and you talk to me about control?'

'Now you're being ridiculous...' Miranda began.

She was given no opportunity to conclude.

'I plead provocation,' he drawled.

This time there was no ferocity. This time his mouth was gentle, leading her, urging her forward, tasting and then withdrawing. Swamped by the new sensations he was evoking, Miranda turned her head, blindly seeking that tantalising touch. There was harshness in the roughness of his unshaven jaw against her tender flesh. But there was no harshness in the way he held her...

No harshness either in the gentle expertise with which he lowered her towel a little to give him access to her vulnerable throat, her breasts. Miranda's head fell back. It was only when she felt the scrape of his unshaven jaw against the softness of her breast that she realised what she was inviting. Her head reared up with a gasp. Horrified, she began to push him away.

Just for a second he resisted her frantic hands. Then, with an audible sigh and a shrug, he released her and stepped back.

Miranda pulled the towel back round her with hands that shook. She did not know what was happening. But she knew she hated him for making her feel like this. For making sure she knew that he knew exactly how he had made her feel. She might be inexperienced but she knew when a man was taunting her. She glared, hating him.

He watched her attempts to restore her modesty without expression. One eyebrow flicked up as if he expected her to hurl accusations at him. But Miranda was too shaken to say anything. He waited. Miranda could not sustain that cynical look of expectation. She dropped her eyes, readjusting her towel with fingers that shook.

At last he gave a soft laugh and went to the door.

'A small illustration of what could happen if the volcano goes up,' Paul Branco said coolly. 'Goodnight.'

He closed the door soundlessly behind him.

* * *

Miranda was too tired not to sleep. But she had turbulent dreams. Several times she came half awake, thinking she was still in that tent, curved against Paul's unresponsive back. Then she thought she was in Bluebeard's castle with someone trying to break into her room. The noise was violent, shaking her out of her half-sleep.

She came up on one elbow, peering anxiously at the door. But the noise came again. It was only the wind, making the ancient timbers of the house creak. She subsided, her heart thundering. In her dream she had been quite convinced that the man outside the door was an enemy; a man who knew her better than she knew herself and was ruthlessly prepared to use that knowledge for his own dark purposes. A man who had power over her.

Miranda put a hand to her throat to ease her breathing.

This is nonsense, she told herself firmly. You're truly safe for the first time in several days and you're creating monsters out of shadows.

A reproachful mew came from the side of the bed. Miranda jumped and then, realising that she had company and it was no terrifying stranger, turned and peered over the side of the bed.

In the darkness she could make out the small shape. The mew came again. It was a good deal louder this time. There was a distinctly commanding note in it.

'You scared too?' she murmured.

She put a hand down and stroked the small head. The cat responded politely but there was no doubt that that was not what he wanted. He scampered to the door. Miranda could hear him scrabbling suggestively.

She groaned. 'Oh, no. You don't want to go out. Tell me you don't want to go out,' she begged.

The paws redoubled their activity on the polished floor.

Miranda gave in. 'Oh, very well. I suppose you have your rights as well as everyone else,' she said with a sigh.

She climbed across the huge bed and found a bedside light. The kitten danced back to her, satisfied. Miranda stood up groggily and looked round.

On either side of the bed there were tall floor-to-ceiling shutters. She pondered. They would almost certainly lead to a balcony of some sort, she thought. If she opened the shutters it would give the kitten access to the outside which he clearly required. It would also mean she did not have to trail through that populous kitchen again.

With some effort, she dealt with the heavy shutters. The kitten was interested. He was not keen on the wind that ruffled his fur, though. Miranda shivered a little at it herself.

She picked him up gently and went out on to the balcony with him. She was stumbling with tiredness, still not entirely awake. She looked round for a safe place for the kitten.

The pale light from the bedside lamp showed a wide, tiled veranda that ran the whole side of the house at first-floor level. At one corner she detected a stairway to the garden. She took the kitten in that direction, stroking the top of his head between the ears as he shivered in the night wind.

At the far end of the terrace there was another lighted window. Neither shutters nor curtains were closed. Miranda could not help seeing its occupants as she passed.

It was a bedroom very like the one she was occupying. Clearly the woman she had seen downstairs, the one who had stood so close to Paul with his arm round her waist, was staying the night. She had changed out of her shirt and trousers now, though. She was wearing a slim satin nightgown that looked as if it might slither off her perfect figure at any moment. And she was brushing her long blonde hair, talking to someone out of Miranda's vision.

The kitten began to struggle. She put him down at the top of the stairs, hardly taking her eyes from the silent tableau beyond the window.

As Miranda watched, caught in spite of herself, it became apparent that the lovely blonde's companion was a man. A tall figure came into view. She could not see his face. He was in his shirt-sleeves, moving with the confidence of a man to whom the woman's bedroom was familiar.

Miranda drew back at once, flattening herself against the wall. The couple were talking easily. The woman was as unembarrassed by his presence as he was. Miranda saw it with an odd little pang she did not understand. Once the woman flung back the long, lovely throat and laughed.

The man seemed to be amused too. He bent and kissed the graceful curve of the woman's shoulder, ruffling her blonde hair. Miranda found that she did not want to know who he was with quite startling intensity. But before she could avert her eyes, he strolled to the window and began to close the shutters. She froze.

The kitten pattered up to her. He had clearly taken advantage of one of the big troughs of flowers to relieve himself, rather than venturing into the wind-swept wastes of the garden. The small imperative mew was loud enough to have Miranda pick him up and hush him, one finger on his nose. He liked that game. He put up a paw and started to dab her finger away from his nose, wriggling with pleasure.

As she rose from her stooping position she had a very clear picture of the man outlined against the lighted window. It was Paul Branco.

Clutching the kitten to her neck, she ran back to her own room. She was shaking again. So much indeed that she could barely close the catch on her own window.

That laughing kiss, that casual ease of intimacy, had shocked her profoundly. Maria Clara's magazines or not, she thought wryly, she had not been prepared for the sight she had just witnessed. Of course that was partly because she felt she had, however involuntarily, been spying on people who thought they were alone. That was enough to make anyone uncomfortable, Miranda assured herself.

Yet she knew it was more than that. The sight of Paul Branco and the blonde woman had stirred something cold and fierce, long dormant, inside Miranda. And it had shaken her to the heart.

Why? She asked herself the question again and again, huddling her arms across herself as she rocked backwards and forwards on the tumbled bed. Was it because she had never seen sophisticated adults with their hands on each other before? Was it because a couple of hours earlier Paul Branco had been kissing her, Miranda? At the thought Miranda pressed the back of her hand to her mouth until the knuckles were bruised against her teeth.

That was impossible. She told herself it was impossible again and again. She might be innocent to the point of naïveté, as he obviously thought, but she was not a fool. If Paul Branco kissed her it was not because he wanted her. Or at least not as he wanted the blonde woman. Not as an equal; not as a lady who had the knowledge of experience and, therefore, the right to invite a man to make love to her. It was precisely because she lacked that knowledge that Paul Branco had been warning her not to give out signals she did not understand.

She ought to be grateful for that warning, Miranda thought. Only... she had a dark suspicion that, in addition to that warning, Paul Branco had made her a present of knowledge that, although she did not yet quite know what it was, would prove more disturbing than all her adventures in the forest.

And I said I wanted adventure, Miranda thought with painful irony. She drifted off into a heavy sleep.

She did not even wake when the heavy door was pushed open with a creaking of hinges. When a tray was placed heavily on the bedside table, she turned, mur-

muring. But she only came awake, blinking, when Anna flung wide the shutters to let in the morning sun.

'Maria Clara?' Miranda said sleepily.

The woman came back to the bedside. 'Chocolate,' she said briefly. 'And clothes. Senhorinha Bebel left some for you. The *senhor* says you are to rest this morning. He will see you at lunch.'

She left before Miranda was awake enough to quibble.

When she had finally got up and dressed in a borrowed blouse and skirt, however, the first person she encountered was not the high-handed master of the house but Lotte Meyer.

Miranda was looking for a couple of new elastic bands to confine her hair in short plaits, to replace the ones that had stretched to breaking-point overnight. She put her head round a door of a room at the end of the downstairs passage and so came face to face with Fräulein Meyer.

The German doctor looked up from a paper she was studying. She had a severe face and a frowning air of abstraction.

'I'm sorry...' Miranda knew at once that she was intruding. It was a sensation she had grown used to, living with Harry. 'I was looking for something to tie up my hair.'

The woman continued to frown at her. Then an expression of comprehension came into her eyes.

'Of course. Harry's child. Miranda, isn't it? What did you want, child?'

'Elastic bands, if there are any,' Miranda said, indicating her plaits.

'Of course.' The woman rummaged through a papier-mâcheé box on the desk in front of her and produced the desired articles. She came forward, her hand held out. 'Here you are. I must say, I didn't recognise you just for a moment. You're looking different from last night, I must say.' She looked disapprovingly at the brightly coloured print skirt and drawstring muslin blouse. 'I suppose those clothes belong to the Martins woman?'

Miranda shook her head. 'I'm afraid I don't know. Anna—the housekeeper—told me someone had lent them to me but I wasn't awake enough to take in who it was.'

Dr Meyer's lips compressed. 'It would be Isabel Martins. None of the maids would own stuff like that. In the absence of a proper lady of the house, I regret to say the Martins woman spends a great deal of time here.'

Miranda thought, She sounds just like Harry. In the circumstances it was a painful thought.

'Well, it's very kind of her,' she murmured.

Dr Meyer sniffed. 'She can afford it. Her family are wealthy and I don't imagine that Branco is ungenerous.'

Miranda flinched, not just at the implications but at the naked spite in the woman's voice. She said gently, 'It is still very kind of her to lend her clothes to someone she's never even heard of.'

Lotte Meyer gave a harsh laugh. 'Oh, she'll have heard all about you by now.'

Miranda was suddenly still, thinking of the beautiful blonde woman Paul Branco had been with last night. Something tightened painfully in her chest.

'You didn't think he'd behave decently just because he had a house full of refugees, did you?' Lotte said harshly. 'He doesn't care about what other people say or what they think. Surely your father warned you?'

Miranda swallowed an unexpected constriction in her throat.

'As far as I can recall, Harry never mentioned Senhor Branco,' she said quietly.

It was Lotte's turn to stare.

'He's never really mentioned any of the Europeans in the area,' Miranda expanded. 'Except you, of course. I—er—I am not supposed to be in the mission, you know. Harry has always been careful.'

Lotte laughed. 'And he didn't warn you about Paul Branco? That doesn't sound very careful to me.' She turned away, her face disturbed. 'Typically male,' she said in disgust. 'If you can't deal with it, pretend it isn't there. He knew perfectly well what Branco was like. He thought he was a devil,' Lotte told her. 'Oh, he stayed here sometimes when he was on his way into the forest but it always worried him.'

'In case he was contaminated, no doubt,' said an ironic voice from the door.

They both swung round. Paul Branco was lounging in the doorway. He did not seem offended at what he must have overheard. Rather, he looked amused. Miranda flushed.

Try as she would, she could not help remembering what she had seen from the terrace last night in devastating detail. She looked at his long fingers, recalled how they had curved against the woman's bared shoulder, and looked sharply away.

Lotte, not noticing, regarded him with disfavour.

'And if he did, was that so surprising? Playing cards under his nose. Plying him with alcohol. Keeping that woman here—openly.'

Paul strolled into the room. 'That woman,' he said evenly, 'brought you here through the floods yesterday at great personal risk. A little more respect is called for, I think.'

Lotte snorted. 'Flaunting hussy.'

Paul looked suddenly amused.

'Whatever happened to Christian charity, my dear Dr Meyer?'

The older woman glared at him. 'I am not your "dear". I'm probably the only woman in the territory who can say that, too.'

He laughed aloud. 'I think you overestimate my charm, doctor. As well as underestimating the deterrent effect of the jungle. I'm not exactly fighting them off, you know.'

Miranda, remembering how she had responded to him last night, blushed painfully. He very nearly had had to fight her off, she thought, wincing.

'I never heard that you fought off any halfway decent-looking woman,' Lotte returned.

He propped himself against a bookcase, one hand in the pocket of his casual trousers, and looked interested.

'You've made a study of my life?' he asked politely.

'I haven't needed to.' Lotte was almost shaking with anger, Miranda noticed suddenly. 'It's an open book.'

Paul's mouth slanted in a sardonic expression. Seeing it, Miranda thought that if she were Lotte she would stop there.

'I wouldn't be too sure of that,' he said softly.

'You've never troubled to hide it. That Martins woman. The hussy from Rio. God knows how many others...'

Paul did not move. The wry smile did not change. But somehow Miranda thought he was suddenly not amused any more.

'I'm flattered you take such an interest in my private life,' he said politely. 'I don't see any need to bore my guest with the details, however.' He turned to Miranda. 'How are you feeling this morning?'

Embarrassed, was the true answer. Embarrassed and confused and dangerously tremulous at the sight of him. She was not going to tell him any of that, of course.

She moistened her lips. 'Fine.'

His eyes flickered. 'No scratches? Abrasions? Bruises? Stiffness?'

She shrugged with a little laugh, her eyes not quite meeting his. 'Stiff, yes. Those weren't the ideal conditions for my first horse ride. The odd scratch, I suppose.'

He looked impatient. 'How long since you had a tetanus jab?'

Miranda's eyes widened. 'Not since I was a child, I think. Why?'

He turned to Lotte Meyer. 'You see, there are more immediately significant things to talk about than my sex life, after all,' he told her sweetly. 'See to it before you go, will you?' He turned. 'I'll be in the study if you want me. I'll see you both at lunch.'

Neither of them could think of anything to say, it seemed. He gave a little nod. It was a graceful gesture of thanks for following his orders, Miranda interpreted. It was obvious that it never occurred to him that either of them might not comply, she thought wryly. And, gallingly, he was justified in his confidence.

Lotte did not even complain as she took her off to the makeshift surgery in an outhouse adjacent to the stables. She looked at the scars of the forest and pronounced them trivial. But she gave Miranda the tetanus shot Paul had instructed.

She also showed surprising interest in a small jagged scar on the side of Miranda's neck where one of the razor-leaved branches had caught her unawares.

'Never heard of Paul Branco before, hmm?'

Miranda shook her head, wincing as the witch hazel burned on the wound.

'And what do you think of him, now you have heard of him?' Lotte said in an absent voice. She was applying a small strip of adhesive bandage to the sore place.

Miranda refused to blush. It was easier when Paul Branco was not in the room.

'I think he's very rude and high-handed,' she said with truth.

Lotte stood back, admiring her handiwork. 'And attractive?'

Miranda shrugged, not answering.

'He seems rather protective,' the woman went on. 'Did he take good care of you in the rainforest?'

Miranda said woodenly, 'He took care of both of us.'

'Yes, of course.' Lotte sounded thoughtful. 'I imagine it was a new experience for him.'

Miranda stiffened. 'On the contrary, I had the impression he knew the forest rather well,' she said carefully, not understanding.

Lotte began to put away her instruments, tossing the small ampoule of anti-tetanus vaccine in the bin labelled 'clinical waste'. Suddenly she seemed to make up her mind about something.

She said slowly, 'He's a cynic. You think he's amusing, I've no doubt. Sexy, even. Isn't that the word girls use nowadays? I'm sure you think Paul Branco is sexy. Half the territory would agree with you. They see the wit and—well, you spent the night in the forest with him; I don't have to spell it out. What they don't see is the coldness.'

She looked at Miranda under her eyelids while her hands stayed busy, returning cotton wool and disinfectant to its rightful place.

'He's a deeply cold man. He doesn't care how his actions affect other people. He needs—well, someone to reawaken his conscience. Someone good, innocent; someone he feels responsible for.'

She closed the medicine cabinet with a decisive snap and locked it. She turned back to Miranda.

'He won't find her, of course. A real innocent would run from a man like that. He could hurt her appallingly. It's a shame. There is a lot of good in that man. Underneath the cynicism. A pity.'

Miranda stood up. 'I suppose so.'

Lotte's eyes were very sharp. 'Nothing to do with me, of course. Or you. Lunch?'

Lunch was set out in a small salon overlooking the garden. Paul was not yet there. Anna brought in a tray of drinks and salads, apologising. There were so many people who needed help. The *senhor* was still engaged. He would be with them very shortly.

He came in with the blonde woman whose shutters he had been closing last night. Miranda felt her throat flood with colour.

Lotte Meyer stiffened.

'Hi,' said the blonde easily, unaware of undercurrents. 'I was looking for you, Lotte. Paul says there's no room for you to stay here, I'm afraid. So you'll have to come back in the helicopter with me this afternoon. We'll find someone to put you up in Santa Cruz.'

The doctor frowned blackly. But she did not protest. The woman's words were friendly enough but she sounded firm.

'Then I will go and pack,' she said icily.

She left the room.

The woman sighed. 'I'm not sure that was entirely sensible, darling. She had rather set her heart on staying here till the river fell.'

Paul strolled across to the sideboard and poured out a couple of drinks. He did not ask the woman what she wanted, Miranda noticed. Presumably he knew. Judging by that scene she had witnessed last night, he knew all there was to know about the beautiful blonde.

Nor did he offer a drink to Miranda. Presumably he thought she was too young, she thought, seething.

'Surprise me,' said Paul indifferently. 'She wants to stay here and convert me. She's made it perfectly plain on a number of occasions. She may be an excellent doctor, but frankly, Bebel, I think she's a trouble-maker. I want her out of my house.'

'Well, you've got her out of your house,' the woman called Bebel said soothingly. 'Be philosophical. She's not all that bad and she does good work among the miners.'

'They have my sympathy,' Paul said, swallowing his drink. 'She's walking proof that the brotherhood of man is a fallacy. She was lecturing Miranda on my wickedness this morning.'

For a horrible moment, Miranda thought he had overheard Lotte's remarks in the surgery. She felt as if embarrassment would choke her. Then she realised that he was only referring to the conversation earlier when he had advised Lotte to concentrate on giving her a tetanus shot rather than describing his sex life in detail.

She fought down a blush. When she looked up she found Bebel looking at her shrewdly.

'Her one aim in life seems to be to make me see the error of my ways,' he concluded drily.

'Not much chance of that,' the blonde said cheerfully. She turned to Miranda with a smile. 'I'm Isabel Martins, since Paul seems disinclined to introduce us. I heard about your awful journey. How are you today?'

'Fine,' Miranda said shyly. The woman's smile was full of real warmth and concern. She smiled back at her. 'A few scratches, that's all.'

Instinctively she touched the small plaster patch on her throat. As Lotte's had done, Bebel's eyebrows rose. She looked swiftly at Paul before turning back to Miranda.

'So what do you want to do next? We're overcrowded in the helicopter this afternoon but I'm sure we can get you into Santa Cruz in the next couple of days if you want.'

Miranda shook her head. 'I—it sounds stupid, I know, but I haven't really thought. I mean—everything I've done up to now has been directed by Harry.'

That had been going to change, of course. That was one of the reasons for the recent ferocious fights. But there was no point in telling that to strangers, however sympathetic they were. It was something she and Harry had to sort out when he came back.

There was a quick look of compassion on the beautiful face.

'So you want to wait here for Harry?'

'I—I suppose so.'

Bebel looked again at Paul. Following her eyes, Miranda was surprised to see an odd expression on his face, part rueful, part resigned.

'How do you feel about that, darling?' Bebel asked.

There was a pause. He drained his glass and looked at it for a moment as if it were a crystal ball he was searching for answers. Then he said indifferently, 'Makes no difference to me. There's enough room.' A thought struck him. 'As long as she doesn't try to convert me, of course.'

Bebel laughed. She sounded relieved. She turned back to Miranda.

'Could you manage a solemn vow not to try and convert him?' she invited.

Miranda smiled, shaking her head. 'That's my father's department, not mine.'

'Fine,' said Paul. He went to the drinks tray and poured another drink for himself. With his back to them, he said, 'It's decided, then. She stays at the *fazenda* until Harry comes back and tells her what to do.' His voice, Miranda thought, sounded oddly harsh.

Bebel noticed nothing, though.

'That seems best.' She hesitated and then said gently, 'If Harry were—away for a long time, what would you do? Have you a guardian in Brazil?'

'Guardian?' Miranda was affronted. 'Good grief, no. I'm twenty-three.'

The effect on both of them was remarkable. Bebel looked astonished—almost dismayed, Miranda thought. And Paul splashed his drink as he swung round. The pungent smell of whisky filled the air.

'*Twenty-three*.' Paul uttered an expletive whose meaning a girl of Miranda's sheltered upbringing could only guess at.

For some reason it had the effect of dispelling the vestige of her own embarrassment. She raised her eyebrows in displeasure.

To her surprise he had the grace to apologise. 'I'm sorry. But what the hell does Harry think he's playing at?'

Miranda was bewildered—and offended. 'What do you mean?'

'Keeping you locked up in that mission like something out of a Gothic novel.' He was in a cold rage, his mouth thin with temper. 'Take a look at yourself in the mirror some time.' It was almost savage.

'I don't understand,' she said, even more offended.

She looked at Bebel. But the blonde woman was staring at Paul with an odd expression and offered no help at all.

'You look like a schoolgirl,' he told Miranda brutally. 'You behave like a schoolgirl. Plaits and kittens, God help me. I thought you were about seventeen.'

'What difference does my age make?' she demanded hotly.

His expression was sardonic. 'If you have to ask that it just proves my point. You can't go back to that damned mission. You've got to go somewhere where there are people and do some growing up. Fast.' He seemed to remember they were not alone. 'Tell her, Bebel,' he ordered.

The other woman shook her head slowly. 'I agree it's an odd situation. But I think Miranda is right to wait until Harry is—er—until Harry comes back before she makes any decisions. After all, whatever else happens he won't be able to keep Miranda's existence a secret any more.'

'No.' Paul's tone was grim. 'I shall see to that personally.'

There was something in his voice that made Miranda shiver. She said, 'You're very kind but you don't need to worry about me. Really. I was already thinking about going back to England.'

Bebel looked at Miranda searchingly.

'Have you done anything about it?'

Miranda suppressed a small smile. Endured Harry's hectoring followed by the icy silences, she thought wryly.

'Harry and I were discussing it.'

Paul's expression was full of comprehension. 'You can carry on discussing it here in my house when the old monster turns up,' he said drily. 'Discussions of that kind go better with a bit of moral support, I find.'

Bebel nodded. 'That's a good idea. And let me know if you want me to do anything,' she added. 'I can contact your family or friends in England if you like, for example.'

Miranda thanked her.

At once, as if glad to have one of a huge list of problems solved, Bebel began to talk about the continuing rescue work. That saw them through Lotte's disapproving return and the whole of lunch, right to the point of the helicopter's departure.

Paul went out to the machine to hand Bebel up into it, once the rest of the passengers were loaded. He had a few words with the pilot. Miranda saw it from her vantage-point under the canopy of the veranda. It was raining hard again. That and the current caused by the helicopter's rotating blades plastered Paul's hair to his head as he ran back to the house.

He lifted an arm in farewell as the machine lifted off. Miranda winced at the noise.

Paul came back laughing. In spite of the rain, which had soaked his shirt and trousers and was running in rivulets down his face, he looked more alive than any human being she had ever seen, Miranda thought. He was like a fire. If you stood too close to him, he scorched you.

He detected something equivocal in her expression.

'What's the matter?'

Miranda shook her head quickly. 'Nothing.'

'Worried about being left alone here with me?'

She stared. 'Alone? But Anna... the maids... Have they gone?'

He chuckled, brushing the raindrops away from his cheekbones with the back of a hand.

'No, they're still here. But I doubt if Dr Meyer counts them in her search for chaperons.'

'*What*?'

'That's what's bothering you, isn't it?' he said shrewdly. 'I saw her corner you before she left.'

Miranda flushed. Lotte Meyer had indeed cornered her—to remind her of Harry's mistrust of Paul Branco coupled with the fact that—under the influence of the right woman—Paul was not beyond salvation.

'She feels responsible, I think. As she was one of the few people who knew I existed.'

'She feels it would be good fun to interfere,' Paul said coolly. 'Don't listen to her. You've had one obsessed autocrat messing up your life. Don't invite another in.'

'Harry hardly messed up my life,' Miranda said quietly.

'No?' His voice was hard suddenly. 'You wanted to live in hiding in the jungle while the rest of your generation were educating themselves with universities and parties and overseas travel?'

Miranda shook her head. 'Not exactly. But it was my choice to come out here, don't forget. I was unhappy in my uncle's house and what Harry offered—seemed worthwhile.'

Until you found the affection was an illusion, she thought sadly. Until you found out that what he was offering was duty and complete intellectual submission and that the love was a fancy in your own head. She turned away.

'It just didn't work out, that's all. It's not Harry's fault,' she said painfully.

Paul made an abrupt movement, abruptly stilled.

'And he took your decision to leave philosophically?'

Miranda sighed. 'He hasn't accepted it yet,' she admitted.

'That must make for a peaceful life,' Paul observed. 'In my experience Harry is as persistent as he is barmy. I imagine you've been quarrelling solidly ever since you made your decision.'

Miranda laughed a little. 'You don't quarrel with Harry Lane. You do what he says. Or he ignores you.' She gave a soft chuckle. 'He's spent a lot of his time ignoring me lately.'

Paul was staring at her. 'Dear God,' he said at last.

She detected criticism of Harry and glared at him. 'You don't understand. I know I haven't been to parties and university and things. I expect you think I'm awfully inexperienced. But it's not been all bad. It's taught me to work things out for myself. And trust myself.'

He said nothing. The defiance dropped from her.

'Just sometimes it got a little lonely,' she admitted.

He searched her face. 'Lonely?'

'For a companion,' Miranda said in a rush. She had no idea why she was telling him this. It slightly appalled her that she was. She had never told anyone else, not even Maria Clara. 'Someone to share things with,' she blurted out. 'Someone to laugh with. Someone who didn't act like a judge all the time.' She stopped herself. 'No, that's self-pitying nonsense. Harry only acts like a judge sometimes.' She thought about it. 'But I used to have this idea that there was someone in the world who would—oh, I don't know—enjoy being with me. Have fun with me. Share things with me.' She looked down, twisting her hands together, shy and furious with herself. 'Oh, it must seem like a lot of nonsense to you,' she muttered.

The dark eyes were brilliant. He stopped brushing the water away from his face. He scanned her expression like a hidden camera. Although she could not look at him, Miranda felt his eyes on her as if he touched her with that fire of his. There was a long silence.

Then, 'No,' Paul said sombrely. 'No. You're talking about the loneliness of the soul. It's a condition I am not unfamiliar with. But what you won't know is that you can feel like that in the middle of a crowded city, Miranda. Maybe more in the middle of a crowded city.

It won't go away just because you leave the jungle. It may even get worse.'

She was startled. She did look up then.

'Believe me,' he said quietly.

CHAPTER FIVE

SOMETHING curious happened then. Even Miranda, all too aware of her inexperience, recognised it. Their eyes locked.

Paul looked like the devil he had called himself, she thought in confusion. The heavy rain had darkened the crisp hair to shiny black. The arrogant bone-structure was very evident under the film of sweat and tropical rain. His eyes were narrowed against the raindrops on the end of his lashes——

Narrowed and fixed on her with a strange intense expression that made something begin to flutter urgently inside her. She felt the rhythm of her breathing accelerate. It startled her and made her uncomfortable. She put a hand to her throat.

Paul continued to stare at her in silence. He looked almost shocked, she thought; shocked and angry.

Miranda found she wanted to touch his face, smooth the harsh lines from around the intent eyes, brush away the tension from his mouth with her own...

She gasped as the tenor of her own thoughts hit her. What was she thinking about? She had no idea how to deal with a devilishly worldly man like Paul Branco. Her own disastrous first and last attempt at love all those years ago should have warned her. She had neither the experience, the defences nor the resilience to recover from the hurt he would undoubtedly inflict. She was too vulnerable and Paul Branco was too adult.

She said fiercely, 'Don't look at me like that.'

He did not pretend to misunderstand her. He said her name under his breath. But he did not try to touch her.

Miranda turned sharply away from him.

'Why did my father call you a devil?' she demanded.

Paul hesitated. 'Who knows?'

She turned back to him, her eyes hardening. 'You know.'

He shrugged. His mouth tilted in self-mockery.

'We didn't agree on priorities.'

Miranda shook her head, rejecting the evasive answer. 'Why say priorities when you mean standards? Moral standards,' she flung at him.

He inspected her flushed face. 'Is that what I mean?' he said slowly.

'You know it is.' She was scornful.

'An interesting deduction.' His voice was smooth as silk. 'On what do you base it?'

She met his eyes unflinchingly this time. 'The way you have treated me.'

His expression was wry. 'You mean getting you away from a mission house that was about to be engulfed by flood water, when your morally impeccable father had left you alone there to fend for yourself?'

That hurt, as, no doubt, it was meant to. Miranda lifted her chin defiantly, refusing to let him see how the reminder of Harry's indifference affected her.

'I was thinking more of the way you bullied and browbeat me on the way here,' she said. 'Your unspeakable arrogance. Your rudeness. Especially last night.'

'Ah.' She glared at him. Paul Branco gave a soft laugh. 'So that's it. What's the matter, my sweet?' he said softly, jeeringly. 'Are you angry with me because I kissed you last night? Or because I didn't take it any further?'

Miranda gasped. For the first time in her life she felt such a surge of fury that, for a few seconds, she literally could not see the man in front of her for the red mist before her eyes.

'How dare you?'

'Oh, I dare,' Paul said coolly. 'The point is, do you? I don't think so somehow.'

'*What*?'

He took her by the upper arms. His grasp was not gentle.

'Listen to me, Miranda.' His voice was grim. 'You're young and you've been living a crazily unnatural life for the last five years. I'm willing to make allowances for that. But you're not a child, no matter what Harry Lane may have told you. You can't behave like a child any more.'

Miranda glared at him. She was outraged.

'What do you mean?' she said, hating him.

'I mean that I need a jumpy adolescent female like I need a hurricane,' he said brutally.

She was speechless.

'Face it. I'm no saint and you're a whole jumble of sexual feelings waiting to find an object. Passionate too, I would say,' he added in a light, indifferent voice that made Miranda want to hit him more than she had ever wanted anything in her life before. Unseen, she clenched her hands till the nails scored the soft palms. 'You're late to start experimenting, too. I can sympathise. Just don't experiment on me.'

Miranda took a hasty step forward. She was burning with shame but indignation was even stronger.

'Are you saying it was I who kissed *you* last night?' she demanded in a voice thick with rage.

For a moment Paul looked startled. His hands fell away.

'No,' he said evenly. 'That was in the nature of a warning. I told you. As I said, I'm no saint. And there is a chemistry between us. Strong chemistry, I suspect.'

Miranda was shaken. She made a small, inarticulate sound.

Paul went on swiftly, 'Don't look like that. It's nothing unusual. If you'd lived in the real world, you'd know it happens all the time. That's why you need to experiment. To sort out the good chemistry from the bad.' He sounded weary. 'Just do me a favour and don't start until you get out of here.'

Miranda could have screamed. '*I* didn't start anything,' she shouted.

He stepped away from her, his expression wry. 'Not intentionally, I agree. But you did.'

'How?' she challenged him.

He looked at her levelly. 'You can dress as a boy, you can put your hair in little girl's plaits and wear clothes that are too big for you; it doesn't change the way you move.' Miranda stared. 'Or the way a man reacts to it,' Paul Branco said deliberately.

She flushed brilliantly. Her eyes fell under his steady regard. Tears rose. She dashed them away angrily.

He took a step towards her, then stopped abruptly. She thought she heard him swear under his breath.

She swallowed the tears and lifted her chin haughtily. 'Why on earth didn't you let me leave with Senhorinha Martins, if you felt like that?' she demanded in a voice that shook.

Paul sighed. 'They were dangerously overloaded as it was.'

'Lotte Meyer didn't want to go,' Miranda pointed out. 'I could have gone in her place.'

There was a tiny pause, then, 'She's got a heart condition,' he said fluently. 'Bebel wanted her near a hospital in case there was a problem.'

There was something in his tone which made Miranda feel she did not know whether to believe him. But, she told herself, if she did not, what reason could he possibly have for keeping her at the *fazenda*? Everything he had said to her made it clear that he wanted her out of his way as soon as possible.

Before she could challenge him, however, he was saying grimly, 'But as soon as the emergency cases are dealt with, you'll be the first on the helicopter to Santa Cruz, believe me.'

There was a call from within the house. He turned his head, running his fingers through his soaking hair.

To her horror and astonishment, Miranda felt her heart shake at the gesture. A surge of longing shot through her. It made her wince and avert her eyes. Maybe Paul Branco knew what he was talking about when he said there was strong chemistry between them, she thought, appalled. It was humiliating.

She said in a harsh voice she barely recognised, 'And in the meantime I'll keep out of your way.'

He looked back at her. There was a glint of amusement in his eyes. She hated the cynical look she saw there.

'You can try.'

But before she could demand elucidation of that either, he was off in answer to that call. His boots clipped sharply on the stone floor as he hurried away. Miranda was left looking after him in mingled anger and trepidation.

She followed him slowly into the house.

She did not see him for the rest of the day. She did not have to make any attempt to keep out of his way either. He was out on the plantation, Anna told her, looking for the injured and people who had been flooded out of their homes.

All through the day they arrived at the *fazenda*, bedraggled, bewildered, exhausted and hopeless. Anna kept the kitchen continuously ready to feed them. Miranda volunteered to help and Anna accepted with only a token protest. It was clear that she was nearly exhausted herself. The stream of refugees showed no signs of letting up.

'It's going to be bad again tonight,' Anna said with a glance out of the window at the gunmetal clouds.

Miranda's heart sank. 'How can you tell?'

'I can't,' Anna said frankly. 'It was in the *senhor's* last note.' She indicated a couple of new arrivals, huddled in blankets over their bowls of *feijoada* 'The Monteiro brothers brought it. He is going out to the Galicia creek to see if anyone has been stranded. He does not expect to be back tonight.'

Miranda shivered. She would not willingly go out in that windy waste again herself. He might be a cynic, she reminded herself, but Paul Branco was a brave man as well. He was out there in this terrible weather trying to save the lives of people he hardly knew. As he had saved her own. It made it puzzlingly difficult to hate him as much as she knew it would be wise to. She shivered again.

Anna looked at her with a good deal of sympathy.

'He will be all right, the *senhor*. He has done this many times,' she said, misinterpreting Miranda's expression. 'Always when people are lost in the forest they call on him. He can take care of himself.'

'I'm sure he can,' Miranda snapped. 'I've never met such a self-sufficient man in my life. Self-sufficient, cynical and with an ice cube for a heart.'

Anna's eyes went to the ceiling. 'Hmm,' she said noncommittally. 'Well, there's no telling when he'll be back. So you'll be on your own for dinner. What time would you like it?'

But Miranda spurned the very thought of dinner. She did what she could to help with the refugees, distributing blankets and dry clothes under Anna's direction. When it was clear that she could do no more without ruining Anna's system, she left the kitchen and roamed restlessly through the main house, looking into empty rooms, pulling books from shelves, unable to settle.

At last she went back to her own room. She could not sleep, she knew, but at least she could play with the kitten. He had appropriated her bed for his daytime slumbers.

But the moment she went in she saw a pale envelope on the bedside table. Her heart stopped. Could Paul Branco be writing to her? Did he regret his harshness, his cynicism? Did he want to tell her things he could not say to her face?

The thought was strangely alarming. Miranda advanced on the envelope as if it were a sleeping anaconda. The kitten lifted its head and watched her sleepily.

She picked up the envelope and scanned it. It was addressed in a neat, rather old-fashioned hand that Miranda was almost certain could not belong to impatient, arrogant Paul Branco. It was reassuring in one way. It was also disappointing. Displeased with herself for that equivocal reaction, Miranda slit the thing open quickly.

She turned it over to inspect the signature. It was from Lotte Meyer. She frowned.

My dear girl,
I feel very uneasy about leaving you alone at the Fazenda Branco. Anna Santos is a good woman but she is devoted to Paul Branco. He is not to be relied on. I feel that in the absence of your father it is my duty to warn you.

Miranda gave a derisive snort. So Lotte was warning her too. She wondered what the missionary would think if she knew that Paul Branco's warning had come first — and been graphically illustrated.

She turned Lotte's letter over. The writing got sharper, more precise, as if the writer had been weighing her words carefully.

'I know your father thinks Paul Branco is a wicked man,' Lotte continued.

Miranda gasped. The letter dropped out of her suddenly slack hands. 'A wicked man'. She could hear Harry saying it. That was what she had tried to remember in the rainforest when Paul had told her that the map was his. She had known there was something. Now it was coming back. She reached back in memory.

'A professional seducer.' That was what Harry had said.

Miranda shivered. She could imagine it all too easily. Except that Paul Branco had not tried to seduce her, had he? He had warned her. And in warning her had showed her, with terrifying explicitness, how easily she could succumb if he did.

Not only a professional seducer but one whom his family had cast off. Paid off, if Harry was to be believed, in order to keep out of Rio. The Fazenda Branco was presumably the price.

Some price, thought Miranda wryly, looking round at furnishings bought by three generations who had not even considered the cost. What on earth had he done?

She went back to Lotte's letter.

'After that business with his sister in law, no woman's reputation is safe with him.'

His sister-in-law? Miranda felt numb.

'He has no respect for innocence. He has already exposed you to gossip by keeping you out for the night in the jungle. Branco will not care, of course. He does not care what people say about him. But your father will care and so will other people. So please be careful, my dear child. You will make choices in the next few weeks that will affect your whole life. If you choose wrongly you will have to pay for the rest of your life.

The signature was an agitated scrawl.

His sister-in law! Miranda shook her head. But he was not like that. He was a hard man, a mocking, mercilessly unsentimental man. But he was not a cheat. She knew, in her heart of hearts, that he was not a cheat.

So, if it were true, and both Harry and Lotte Meyer seemed to take it as beyond doubt, then there could only be one reason for it.

'He must have been terribly in love with her,' she said aloud.

And so the family had rejected him.

The letter fluttered to the floor as Miranda stood up and went to the window. She knew something about family rejection. She was not inclined to condemn Paul Branco out of hand because of that alone. And for the rest, all that Lotte could accuse him of was not caring about what people said about him.

Yet the message was not so different from what Paul himself had said. And Miranda had seen the cynicism for herself. What on earth had made him like that? she wondered. The relationship with his brother's wife? It was an oddly painful thought.

She moved restlessly, looking out into the rain-filled blackness.

Was he out there somewhere, cold and tired? Or had he pitched his tent and brewed beans for one of his orphans of the storm as he had done for her?

An unexpected gust of emotion, like a pain, shook her at the thought. Miranda gave a gasp. She stepped back from the window as if it had burned her. She was shaking, she found.

'Jealousy,' she said aloud. 'I'm jealous. How can I be jealous? Oh, lord, what is *happening* to me?'

She gathered up the sleepy kitten and almost fled from the room.

Which was why, when Paul came into the drawing-room an hour later, he found her curled up in an armchair, reading a battered paperback novel.

He stopped at the sight of her, a curious expression crossing his face. Miranda lifted her head. Meeting his eyes, she flushed slightly.

But all she said was, 'Are you all right? How was it?'

He shrugged, going to the drinks tray.

'Wet and wild. Everyone at Galicia Creek seemed to have got away before the river started to rise.' He poured himself a generous drink. 'There was no sign that Harry had been there.'

'Oh.' Miranda jumped. It had not occurred to her that he would be looking for her father. 'D-did you think he would be there, then?'

Paul turned with a glass in his hand. 'You don't know him very well, do you?' he said in a curious voice.

Miranda detected criticism. She lifted her chin. 'I know him as well as he permits,' she said with dignity.

'Yes, I suppose you do.' He looked down at the pale gold liquid in his glass, swirling it round thoughtfully. 'He didn't tell you anything? About what he was doing or where he was going, I mean?'

Miranda shook her head. 'Nothing. He said what I didn't know I didn't need to waste my time thinking about.' She laughed suddenly. 'Harry is very hot on people not wasting time. He thinks I spend too much time telling the children stories and not enough teaching them geography. And as for listening to the stories they tell me—well, that's pure trivia.'

Paul smiled absently. His eyes searched her expression. 'And he never mentioned me?'

Miranda shook her head again. 'I told you. He didn't tell me anything. I think he's afraid I'll use it against him,' she added, her tone unconsciously wistful. 'Harry says the world is full of betrayers.'

'Including you?' Paul sounded incredulous.

Miranda bit her lip. Her father had not begun to be suspicious of her until she had told him she wanted to leave the little mission. That she felt trapped. That she desperately needed to see the outside world again. That was when he had started to hide things from her.

She said carefully, 'He is becoming very intolerant of people who do not share his views in every respect.'

Paul gave a soft laugh. '"Becoming"? I don't ever remember him as the tolerant type.'

Miranda was curious. 'How long have you known him?'

'Longer than you if you only met him five years ago,' Paul said wryly. 'He moved into the territory about fifteen years ago, I suppose. I didn't own the place in those days, of course. I just used to bump into him, tearing up the rainforest to grow tomatoes.' He showed his teeth in a brief, harsh smile. 'I dissuaded him.'

Miranda was impressed. She had never managed to dissuade Harry from doing anything he wanted to in all the time she had spent with him. She said so.

Paul propped himself against the mahogany table and eyed her curiously.

'Why did you come out here, then?' he said abruptly.

She was unprepared for the curt question. It made her heart lurch.

'It's a long story,' she said evasively.

Paul looked out at the blackness beyond the French windows. The wind was rising again, making the bougainvillaea against the house rattle like a troop of skeletons. His mouth tilted.

'It's going to be a long night. And I'm not going anywhere.'

Miranda looked at him. He had one hand in the pocket of his chinos, the loose cotton jacket pushed back casually. Trousers, shirt and jacket were all stained with vegetation and marks where the tropical downpour had soaked them and then dried out. Clearly he had not shaved since the morning and his jaw was dark with the day's growth of beard. He looked a complete ruffian—tough and capable and faintly frightening. The most frightening thing of all was the teasing warmth in the eyes resting on her as he waited for her answer.

With a slight shock Miranda realised how very attractive the ruffian was. She corrected herself—how very attractive he was to her.

She swallowed.

'Well?' He was watching her lazily. 'You were—what? Eighteen? A bit late for running away from school. So what were you running from?'

She jumped and her heart began to beat lightly and hard somewhere up in her throat. Oh, he saw everything, this laughing, careless ruffian.

'How do you know I was running from anything?' she demanded stiffly.

'Harry must have been a hard pill to swallow unless you were desperate,' he said cynically. 'So what was it? Bad exam results? Teenage love-affair that went wrong?'

She said nothing. She was sure she did not even move. But his eyes sharpened.

'So that's it.' He drained his glass, watching her. 'What did the boy do? Stand you up on a date? Wasn't Harry and the Amazon jungle rather a drastic solution?' The lazy, amused drawl infuriated Miranda. Which was just as well. It got her past the crippling embarrassment. She looked at him with dislike.

'The *boy* lived in the same house as I did and thought I should become his mistress,' she said with precision.

Paul's eyebrows flew up in undisguised astonishment. That gave Miranda a little satisfaction. So he did not know everything there was to know about her after all, she thought.

'Whenever his wife was away,' she ended frostily.

He recovered his cool at once. He put his glass down.

'Unpleasant,' he said with a neutral voice. 'I suppose you were in love with him.'

In spite of herself Miranda flushed miserably. He gave that lop-sided smile that expressed as much cynicism as amusement.

'Of course you were. Declarations of love are heady stuff when you're eighteen. However illicit.' His voice was meditative. 'I still think the Amazon was drastic.'

She shrugged. 'My mother died when I was twelve. I'd lived with my uncle's family ever since. They were kind enough but—oh, you know. They didn't know what to do with me. I didn't have any money and they had lived way beyond their income so I was a burden they could do without. When Harry came along with his proposal that I join him...' She shrugged again. 'Well, Harry was my father. He said he loved me and it was time we got to know each other. It seemed meant, somehow.'

There was a little silence, then Paul said expressionlessly, 'I can see that it would.' He turned his back on her and refilled his glass. 'When did you find out that it was less than ideal?'

Miranda thought about it. 'It's hard to say. It wasn't what I expected—but then I didn't know what to expect so that didn't really worry me. I liked teaching the children. And I liked the other people at the mission.' She paused. 'I think that was it...the way Harry never— never *respected* anyone else. There was an anthropologist staying at first. He was the man who showed me your map. Harry threw him out as soon as he found out.'

'Rolf Pulos,' Paul said. 'I wondered why he never mentioned you. I suppose Harry sent him on his way before he had the time.'

Miranda's eyes widened. 'Was that why he was so mad at my seeing the map?'

'I imagine so.' Paul's tone was even but she had the impression that there were strong feelings underneath banked down quite deliberately.

She sent him a cautious look.

'So who else?' he demanded. 'There was Harry and the children and the odd mission servant. Didn't you see anyone else in five years? Not even Lotte?'

Miranda shook her head. 'There was another teacher from the village: Maria Clara. She looked after the smallest ones and used to ferry the children backwards and forwards. She was good fun. Harry said she was frivolous and sent her away.'

'That figures.' It was muttered.

Miranda stared at him. 'What?'

'Never mind. Nothing relevant. What about Lotte?'

'He talks about Dr Meyer,' Miranda admitted. 'He doesn't really approve of her. He thinks she's too inquisitive.'

'That's the only thing I've ever found that Harry and I agree on,' Paul said. 'Given the choice I would never have had the woman in the house. How did you get on with her?'

Miranda considered. 'All right, I think. She did seem very curious about me, though.'

'She would.' He gave a sharp sigh. 'Lord, what did I do to deserve her and Henry Lane in my territory? The brothers at Cuidade Verde are angelic and the medical mission upriver does first-class work. But I get a medieval hellfire preacher and that nosy old crosspatch. Grr.'

He looked so wry that Miranda laughed in spite of herself. It did not seem very loyal to Harry and she stopped at once. But there was undoubtedly more than a grain of truth in his comment.

Paul moved and sat on the arm of her chair. He searched her face. He was casual, swinging one booted foot; but that searching inspection was not casual. The dark eyes were warm again.

'You should laugh more often,' he said at last. 'It reminds one how young you really are. I hope you didn't let her get you down. She has her hobby horses—notably my degenerate lifestyle, as you heard, I'm afraid. But basically she doesn't matter a row of beans. Did she upset you?'

'What?' Miranda jumped. 'Oh, no.'

'Didn't grill you about our unchaperoned night together?'

Miranda was startled. She remembered Lotte's note and flushed uncomfortably. 'Well...'

'Tell me the truth, Miranda,' he said quietly.

She looked down in embarrassment. 'Not exactly. But she did write to me. She said she wanted to—warn me.'

'About me?'

She nodded, unable to speak.

He swore softly. 'I suppose I should have expected something of the kind. In a way the only surprising thing is that she left you here at all. Presumably she thinks a missionary's daughter should be able to resist me,' Paul said drily. 'In fact I wouldn't have been surprised if she had set you on trying to reform me.'

Remembering the hints in the surgery, and the implications of Lotte's note, she winced, her eyes sliding away from him.

SAVING THE DEVIL

Paul misinterpreted the action. Miranda's look of horror set him laughing aloud again.

'Quite right,' he said, flicking her hot cheek with cool fingers. 'Don't try it. I passed the point of redemption a long time ago.'

CHAPTER SIX

BEYOND redemption! Miranda turned the mocking words over and over in her head when she was alone at last in the room that had been allotted to her. Or relatively alone, she thought wryly, as the kitten made a nest in Bebel Martins' discarded print skirt.

Why did Paul Branco tell her so determinedly that he was beyond redemption? Was it merely the impatience of an experienced man who had had too much moral reproach directed at him already from his missionary neighbours? Or was there something more to it? Was he trying, in his own way, to warn her not to involve herself in his affairs?

Miranda remembered the warning he had given her in this very room—and the form it had taken. Was it only last night? Her mouth, her whole skin tingled at the memory. It occurred to her that the warning might have come too late.

She moistened suddenly trembling lips. She looked quickly at the door through which he had come last night. Would he come to her again tonight? And if he did, what would she say? What would she do? What would *he* do? Her heart began to slam against her ribs.

Oh, lord, thought Miranda. This is alarming. Paul himself warned me explicitly not to tangle with him. So too did Lotte when we talked and then when she wrote to me. She gave me more details, more reasons. And I knew the moment I set eyes on him that he was an arrogant bully who didn't care a hoot for anyone's opinion but his own. I *can't* want to get involved with him. Surely I can't? I'm not a fool. Or, at least, I've never been a fool up to now.

She sat on the end of the bed and watched the door. Something deep inside her was quivering uncontrollably. But the big house was silent, except for the wind and rain lashing at the shutters. Paul Branco did not invade her bedroom again.

Eventually she crept under the covers. She curled her knees up tight to her chest, and huddled her arms round them. She told herself she was cold. But it was not a physical cold. When she slept, she dreamed of being in the rainforest again, lost and frightened, searching frenziedly through giant plants that plucked at her face and clothes for something or someone she did not know. And she stayed cold.

The next morning she was up before it was light. The wind had dropped but when she opened her shutters and the window on to the terrace the air had a heaviness to it which Miranda found ominous. She scrambled into the borrowed clothes and ran down the carved staircase.

Paul was crossing the bottom of the stairs. He halted and looked up at her breathless appearance. Miranda thought he looked briefly put out. But when she got closer, she saw that his expression was as cool as ever. So either she had been mistaken or he had schooled his features with lightning speed.

'Good morning. I see you are keeping missionary hours now you've recovered from the jungle,' he teased.

Miranda smiled at him. 'I'm not sure I'll ever recover from the jungle,' she said ruefully. She shook her head, laughing. 'And I was telling Maria Clara only the day before the rains started that I wanted more adventure.'

'Beware of what you wish for; you might get it,' Paul said solemnly.

She sighed. 'Obviously you're right.'

He pinched her cheek lightly. 'Don't look so downcast, my child. It's a useful lesson to have learned. Among others.' His tone was suddenly dry.

Miranda remembered all too vividly the other lessons she had learned at Paul Branco's hands. Her eyes fell. She gave a sweet, secret shiver at the thought.

The long fingers tipped her chin. Paul scanned her face searchingly. The dark eyes were piercing, the handsome mouth set in uncompromising lines.

'Remember them,' he said softly.

So he was thinking of that devastating kiss too, Miranda thought with a little rush of triumph. She veiled her eyes but her pulse was racing. Even though he had gone straight to the beautiful Bebel's room, he had not been able to banish the memory, any more than she had herself. And he did not have inexperience as an excuse.

She stepped back out of the reach of his hands.

'I do,' she said coolly. 'Do you?'

For a moment he looked disconcerted. Then he laughed.

'Good point,' he said. 'You're sharper than you look. I must remember it.'

The look he gave her was speculative. Miranda bit back a smile. No more talk of her youth now, she thought, quietly exultant.

'Yes,' she said. 'You must.'

He laughed suddenly, his eyes dancing. Not for the first time the sheer force of his attraction beat at Miranda like flames from a particularly heated bonfire. She blinked, silenced.

'I will,' he promised. 'Now come and have breakfast with me. Unless missionary's daughters don't eat until the sun is up?'

Miranda laughed and fell into step beside him. The hallway had a small window out to the yard behind the stable. She looked at it and shivered a little.

'Do you think the sun will rise this morning?' she said, trying to make a joke of it. 'It felt very strange when I opened the window. Depressing. Almost—scary.' In spite of herself, she shivered.

Paul sent her a quick look. But he said easily, 'You're suffering from having to wear the same clothes two days running. Every woman I know would find that depressing.'

Miranda shook her head in protest.

'With every justification,' he said firmly.

'Come along. Let's go and find you something else.'

Unselfconsciously he took her hand. Miranda jumped. It was like touching a live wire. How could he not be conscious of it? But he seemed oblivious.

She thought he would take her to the trunks of clothes prepared for the refugees from the storm. But he did not. Instead he took her upstairs again, to a room she had never been in before.

It was astonishing. Miranda stood in the doorway, awestruck at the Second Empire furniture, the elaborate gold and maroon hangings, the carpet that had been, unmistakably, woven to fit just this room and just this furniture.

With the disdain of long familiarity, Paul strode across to the heavy walnut wardrobe and flung it open.

'Grandmama's stuff,' he said. 'She had a hand-span waist and a taste for cloth of gold but there should be something in there you would enjoy wearing.'

He laughed at her bemused expression.

'Find yourself some cloth of gold and I'll make you the best breakfast in the southern hemisphere.'

Miranda went through the clothes with awed fingers. They had been lovingly cared for, in spite of their age. They all had the stamp of quality, some bearing the names of designers that widened her eyes, little though she knew about fashion. In the end she chose a high-waisted skirt that rustled as she walked and a creamy blouse fastened with a thousand little pearl buttons and felt like heaven.

Shyly she went down to the kitchen.

Paul looked round from the range. His eyes widened a little, she thought. But all he said was, 'We seem to have another hand-span waist in residence.'

Miranda refused to blush. She sat down at the kitchen table.

'She must have been very beautiful.'

He raised his eyebrows. 'Because she spent a fortune on her clothes? That's very feminine logic, if I may say so.'

She shook her head, refusing to rise to the bait. 'Because they are very beautiful clothes, very simple.'

He laughed. 'All that means is she had good taste. She was the one who insisted on building this house. She created the gardens here. That's where I inherited it—both the *fazenda* and the know-how.'

'Were you brought up here?'

Paul laughed softly. 'I was brought up in Rio. And Paris. And Washington. When my grandfather died he left it to me for other reasons,' Paul said coolly. 'It really wasn't my father's sort of thing at all. He's a politician. Move him fifty kilometres out of a city and he starts to doubt his existence. Whereas I——'

Miranda looked round the well-fitted kitchen and thought of the untidy crowded corner she had had to cook in at the mission.

'It's not exactly rural simplicity, is it?' she said drily.

Paul looked taken aback. 'Isn't it?'

'Not if you're used to a fifty-year-old draining-board with knot holes,' she told him frankly. 'I've never even imagined the luxury you seem to take for granted.'

'Which all may blow away in the hurricane,' he pointed out. Suddenly his eyes began to dance. 'Since this may be the last day any of this is standing, why don't we breakfast in style? You're dressed for it, after all.'

Miranda jumped. 'Style?' she said suspiciously.

'Follow me.'

She did. He flung open a door to a small room she had not seen before. In the corner of the house, it commanded a perfect view of the gardens, stretching away to the edge of the forest. Miranda went to the window and looked at the distant blackness. She shivered a little, clasping her arms in front of her.

'Forget it,' Paul said behind her softly. 'Enjoy the moment. Sit at my table and I will ask Anna to make us a four-course breakfast, just like my grandparents used to give their guests.'

He was as good as his word. Anna brought them dish after delicious dish of eggs and fruit and home-made bread warm from the oven. Anna beamed, and Paul kept up a gentle, amusing stream of conversation that calmed Miranda and charmed her into forgetting. She forgot the wind and the forest and everything but the man sitting opposite her, with the derisive light banished from his eyes for once.

'It must be wonderful to have been brought up to all this,' she said wistfully, touching the exquisite linen tablecloth Anna had spread for them.

He was peeling a mango, the long fingers deft on a chased-silver fruit knife. He laughed softly.

'I wouldn't know.'

Miranda stared. She looked up to find him watching her. There was something in that steady regard that reminded her of a scientist, adjusting his microscope until he got a magnification that satisfied him.

At last he said slowly, 'You mustn't get the wrong impression of me, Miranda. I'm as much of a displaced person as you are. I've been alone on the roads in foreign countries. I've had so little money that there were times when I only ate when I picked up work on a building site or as a tourist guide.

'Don't look at me like that,' he said, suddenly harsh. 'You look round at the *fazenda* and the mahogany furniture and you think I was born a rich man. You could not be more wrong. My mother was a cabaret dancer and my father did not even acknowledge me until I was ten and my grandfather made him——' He broke off as if he regretted the impetuous confidence. His eyes were nearly black and verging on hostile. But at least he wasn't mocking her any more, Miranda thought, shaken...shaken and oddly exhilarated. Her hand almost went out to him. She bent her head.

'I didn't know,' she admitted in a small voice.

The anger, or whatever it was, seemed to go out of him. He shrugged.

'Why should you? Most people don't. And you, by your own account, did not even know of my existence until three days ago.' He added, 'Don't look like that. It hasn't been a bad life.'

No? Miranda shook her head. Barely acknowledged by his family, then rejected because he was in love with his sister-in-law. Who presumably had rejected him as well. There was no sign that she had ever been here with him.

'At least Harry never rejected me,' she said impulsively.

Paul flung back his head and laughed.

'Don't turn me into a martyr,' he begged. 'It's bad enough being responsible for a lady out of a fairy-story without you going sentimental on me.'

Miranda sat up very straight all of a sudden.

'Responsible for...? What are you talking about?' she gasped.

He handed her a chunk of mango. She ate it absently.

'Of course I'm responsible for you,' he said calmly. 'I made myself responsible the moment I wouldn't let Heitor ride off with you.'

Miranda's chin lifted sharply. 'Neither you nor anyone else is responsible for me,' she announced coldly.

His smile slanted. He did not otherwise answer.

She pounded her fists on the crisp embroidered linen. 'You're not.'

'If only I weren't,' he said softly, but with unmistakable feeling.

Miranda was silenced. She watched him resentfully as he poured more coffee from the pot Anna had brought in. He pushed the tiny cup across the table to her.

'Drink your *cafezinho*,' he said with odious patience. 'Maybe it will sweeten your temper.' He looked at his watch. 'At some time we will have to discuss what's to be done about you, missionary's daughter. But not now. I'm meeting Heitor up on the ridge at first light. You've nearly made me late already.'

He came lightly to his feet, looking down at her with a mocking smile. Miranda glared. The smile slanted more acutely. He touched his fingers fleetingly to the space between her eyebrows.

'Don't frown at me like that,' he said softly. 'No one else even comes close to making me late.'

She gasped, totally taken aback. But before she could demand an explanation, he was gone. She drank the fierce coffee he had given her. It tasted foul, she thought.

Paul did not return for the rest of the day. Miranda, hovering anxiously in the kitchen, overheard the messages that his manager, Rubem, picked up on the radio and relayed to Anna. They were brisk and factual and not one of them mentioned Miranda.

She helped in the kitchen, chopping vegetables and minding simmering pots, but none of it took her mind off what he had said. She was consumed with restlessness. What had he *meant*?

'Where is he now?' she asked Anna impatiently as the light began to fall again. 'Isn't he even coming home tonight?'

Anna looked worried. But she said soothingly, 'I'm sure he will if he can.'

'And what about your wonderful supper?' Miranda raged, although she knew it was ridiculous. 'You take all that trouble to cook for him and he can't even be bothered to let you know whether he will be home to eat it.'

Anna's broad face took on a look of amusement.

'Times like this you keep food hot all the time. A man eats when he can.'

'But——'

Anna looked out of the window, her pleasant face bleak suddenly. 'That's a bad storm coming. Rubem says the river is rising again. That's why they've been trying to get everyone down into Santa Cruz before it hits.'

Miranda had been vaguely aware of the helicopter arriving and departing all afternoon. Now she realised that the only people left in the kitchen were the *fazenda's* maids. She swallowed.

'Are we in danger?' she said in a small voice.

'Here?' Anna shook her head. 'Too high. River never rises up this far. We could be cut off for a while.' She looked troubled. 'I wasn't sure whether you should go back to Santa Cruz as well when the last helicopter went. It won't be back soon if there's more storm damage. But Senhorinha Martins said you were better off at the *fazenda* and the *senhor* agreed so I didn't say anything to Rubem. I hope the *senhor* won't be angry with me when he finds out, though.'

Her pleasant face said that she was not at all sure.

Nor, when Miranda turned from her anxious scanning of the blackness outside and saw him striding through the kitchen door, was she.

'You're back,' she said, preparing herself for battle. If he was going to complain about finding her here after the mass evacuation, she was going on the offensive first. 'It's been a long time since you called in,' she reminded him harshly. 'Was it an emergency?'

His mouth was grim. He looked appallingly tired, she thought suddenly. Under the mud stains of the day, the tanned skin looked grey with fatigue. He passed a hand over his eyes.

'You might say so. I've got some bad news, I'm afraid.'

Miranda stared at him. Bad news? Had the river burst its banks? The Range Rover finally got bogged down in mud? And then, meeting his eyes and seeing the compassion in them, she understood. Her heart contracted.

'Harry,' she said in rusty whisper.

His mouth twisted. 'I'm afraid so.'

Both her hands went to her mouth in tight fists, pressed against her lips. 'Oh, *no*.'

'There's no good way to say this,' Paul sounded angry. 'He'd tried to take the boat into a creek. It seems to have overturned. We got him out tonight. He would have drowned very quickly. Miranda, I'm sorry.'

She felt numb.

'That's all right. I'm sure you did your best.' Her voice was polite.

He looked even more grim. He took her by the shoulders, his eyes boring into hers. He curved a hand round her cheek, brushing at the flyaway strands that still escaped the confines of Lotte's elastic bands.

'Don't be so calm. Cry. Scream at me,' Paul urged huskily. 'Anything. Give vent to your feelings. Don't bottle them up.'

Miranda shook her head. She did not know what to say. She did not even know what she felt, she thought remotely. He searched her face. She did not try to hide her feelings from him. Chiefly, she thought, they were a sort of frozen bewilderment.

'Say something, Miranda,' he said at last gently. 'Whatever you think of me, this isn't the time to suppress what you feel.' He stroked her hair a couple of times. 'I won't hold it against you. You can go back to shouting at me afterwards. Just don't shut me out now.'

She swallowed. 'I'm not sure what I feel,' she managed at last. Her voice sounded odd. 'I—I don't seem to feel anything very much.'

'Shock. Of course. I'm a fool.' He slipped one arm round her shoulders. 'Come into the drawing-room and I'll give you a stiff drink.'

She went with him obediently. She knew he was looking down at her in concern. But she still could not speak. He poured her brandy without asking, pressing the balloon glass into her hand and closing her fingers round it.

'Drink,' he said curtly.

Still silent, she obeyed. But after a mouthful she put the glass down. Paul frowned heavily.

'Oh, no,' she whispered. 'Please. Really, I don't want it.'

He knelt beside her chair and searched her face.

'Coffee, then.'

In spite of the ice inside her, Miranda gave a pale smile.

'A *cafezinho*? Please no. I really don't care for it.'

'That's verging on treason,' Paul said. It sounded as if his effort at normality was as great as hers. 'You must have had coffee at the mission.'

She thought she could detect a note of relief in his voice. He must have wondered if he had a voiceless zombie on his hands forever, she thought.

'Not the way you make it,' she said thinking of the black treacle he had given her at breakfast. 'So strong and sweet.'

'That's how all Brazilians drink it,' he said. 'You must have been insulting your throat with some terrible English brew.'

'No. Harry doesn't like us drinking coffee at all. We always have tea,' she said——

And stopped. The shock was like the pain of stabbing herself with a needle. She drew a shaky breath.

'Didn't. Didn't like coffee,' she corrected herself steadily.

Paul said, 'Oh, my dear.'

He pulled her abruptly into his arms, one hand going to cradle her head against his stained shirt-front.

'Cry,' he commanded.

And suddenly she found that she could.

Miranda cried until she had no tears left. Paul held her the whole time. He made no comment as her shoulders shook convulsively and her feelings exploded in great gulping sobs. The warm chest beneath her cheek felt like a rock.

Eventually she was exhausted. Her sobs dwindled into little choking gasps, and then died away altogether. Her throat felt scratched to ribbons by all the crying. Her eyes were sore and her head ached. But there were no more tears.

Wearily she lifted herself out of Paul Branco's arms. For a moment he resisted the movement. Then, very carefully, he settled her back among the cushions. His arms fell, though he stayed kneeling beside her.

'I'm sorry,' Miranda said. She scrubbed the back of her hand across her eyes and swallowed.

Paul touched the hair back from her damp forehead very gently. Then his hand fell away. He gave her the brandy glass again.

'For what?' he said drily. 'Grieving? We all do that some time, one way or another. Take that drink now.'

Before she could answer he rose lightly to his feet and went to the console table. Miranda saw that he was pouring a drink for himself. He splashed some golden liquid into a glass and tossed it down in one gulp.

He was unshaven again. The darkness of his jaw only accentuated the tense pallor of his face. He looked as if he had been driven to the end of his endurance.

Of course, Paul had probably been working for hours before they found Harry, Miranda thought with sudden compassion. No matter how equivocal his feelings about Harry in ordinary circumstances, he must have felt bitterly defeated when they recovered the poor drowned body. Or maybe more than one. Harry had intended to pick up believers as he went upriver. It was a big boat to sail on your own for any length of time.

'Was he—still alone?' she asked, appalled at the thought.

'Yes, thank God.' Paul poured another glass and drank it as quickly. He was staring in the mirror above the console table but he seemed to be far away; somewhere dark. He gave a shudder. 'Harry didn't try to persuade you to go with him?'

Miranda shook her head. 'He knew I didn't really agree with his missions into the jungle.'

'Thank God for that at least,' Paul said. His voice was almost violent. 'What in *hell* he thought he was doing...'

Miranda made a small, shocked protest.

'I'm sorry.' He sounded impatient. 'But a man with responsibilities has no right to go jaunting off into the wilderness trying to interfere with other people's before he's provided for his own.'

'Responsibilities?'

Paul took another drink. He did not swig this one down. Instead he turned sharply, suddenly. He stood there watching her, leaning against the table. He cradled the glass against his belt. The long fingers did not look entirely steady, Miranda saw with astonishment. The unsuccessful rescue must have been more physically taxing than she had realised, she thought.

'Responsibilities,' he repeated with deliberation.

She stared. Harry had been conscious of his responsibility to his flock every waking moment. She shook her head in bewilderment. 'But——'

'Like a motherless daughter in a foreign land.' He was curt to the point of rudeness. 'Without money or friends. Or the means of acquiring either.' He sounded furiously angry.

Light dawned on Miranda. Paul had already told her he regarded her as a responsibility. Now that her father was dead he would be even more convinced that he needed to look after her. And he had made no secret of the fact that he did not relish the prospect. She flushed.

'I can look after myself——' she began stiffly, but she was interrupted. Paul gave vent to a truly savage expletive. Miranda blinked.

'You're all right *now*. But what if Heitor and I hadn't come along? What if you were all alone in that blasted schoolhouse? Or in the rainforest on your own? Who would have come looking for you? Who even knew you existed?' he flung at her. 'A handful of children and a couple of Indian workers who can't even write. Even if they knew who to write to. It's a nightmare.' He took a swallow of his drink. His expression was black.

'Oh.' She shook her head slowly. 'I didn't think of that.'

'Fortunately you don't have to.'

She bit her lip. 'Because I'm here in your house, you mean? But I can't trespass on your hospitality...' Her voice trailed off into silence. She sounded miserably prim, she thought, disgusted with herself. Prim and ungracious when all she wanted was to sound coolly in control of her own life.

She tried to repair it. 'Not that I'm not grateful. I know my chances of survival weren't great without you...'

That sounded even worse—almost sulky. Paul looked like thunder. Miranda subsided into despairing silence. She did not entirely blame him. Why, oh, why did he have this effect on her? Nobody else had ever made her so self-conscious that she ended up sounding like a petulant schoolgirl.

His mouth thinned. But all he said was, 'I'm afraid you'll have to trespass on my hospitality, such as it is, for the time being.'

Miranda was about to protest when she was stopped by another painful consideration. She swallowed.

'What has happened to Harry's body?' she said with difficulty. 'I know there'll have to be a funeral. I don't know what the formalities are.'

Paul said gently, 'I will attend to it.'

'But——'

'He is not the only one to die, sadly. Arrangements are in hand.'

'Oh.' Somehow it was a great relief. 'Thank you.'

She sniffed. She found that a handkerchief was being dropped into her hands. It was crumpled and less than immaculate but it served. She accepted it with gratitude. Paul stepped back. Miranda blew her nose vigorously.

'I'm sorry. I didn't mean to start dripping again.'

'Do not apologise. You have reason enough to cry, if anyone has.'

He sounded distant, in spite of the cool kindness of his words. Miranda looked at him under her lashes. He looked tired to death—or as if he was in pain, she thought, startled. He was also standing about as far away from her as he could get without actually putting the furniture in between them, she noticed. It made her feel oddly forlorn, that distance between them.

To disguise it she blew her nose again and stood up briskly.

'Possibly. But not over you. You have already been more than kind.'

He grimaced. 'Kind? Is that what you call it? Miranda, I'm not a kind man. I——'

He was interrupted by noises in the passage outside.

'Damn,' he said under his breath. He pushed a hand through his hair. 'Oh, for some *time*. Look, Miranda, I can't afford any more now. I'm sorry. We will have a long talk, I promise. We'll go through what your options are together. Then I can help you do whatever you decide you want to do. Get a job. Go to university, if you like. Back to England. Somewhere else—the States maybe. But I can't talk about it now.'

Miranda stepped back as if he had thrown up a wall between them. Her chin rose.

'Of course not,' she said with crisp dignity. 'I appreciate how busy you are. It was good of you to take the time to tell me about Harry yourself.'

Paul swore again, startling her. 'I told you I wasn't kind,' he said with a glimmer of smile briefly dispelling the look of strain. 'Believe me, this is no charitable venture on my part. If I hadn't wanted to do it myself,

I would have let someone else tell you about Harry. Bebel would have been better, anyway. But I—wanted to be there for you.'

The dark eyes glittered. He sounded impatient again, almost angry. It confused Miranda. Why did he say— well, as good as say—that he cared about her feelings and then look at her in that fierce way?

And, more important, why did this inexplicable anger send her into such turmoil? She was no coward. Harry had lost his temper with her over and over again and she had only laughed. Yet Paul Branco frowned and her knees turned to water.

Scanning the tense, handsome face, Miranda made a discovery. Her knees might be totally fluid but it was not entirely due to fear. There was excitement there as well. Excitement and a queer cold feeling, curling beneath her breastbone, which she recognised. It was anticipation. That scared her more than all the rest.

She gulped. 'Thank you,' she said.

The noises from the corridor came closer. There was a perfunctory knock on the door and Anna's anxious face appeared.

'Heitor do Campo,' she began. 'The Medical Air Rescue Service say have you seen him?'

There was a fierce explosion of sounds and Anna was pushed unceremoniously aside. Two men, worn and filthy, pushed their way past her, talking hard. Even Miranda, who had got used to the local dialect, found them hard to follow. But one look at Paul's expression made it virtually unnecessary.

'When did he go missing?' he snapped, pushing the half-full glass away from him as if its contents had never held any interest for him. 'Where?'

The men told him as best they could. It was clear that there had been an accident. They had seen Heitor's horse stumble in the mud of a steep forest path. They had caught the horse—it was in the stable, since they had ridden it to the *fazenda* for help—but they had not managed to find Heitor. And soon it would be night.

'Will a four-wheel drive get me there?' Paul said.

The men looked doubtful.

'Perroquet,' Paul said to Anna. 'Lemanja is tired. Have them saddle a couple of fresh horses for these gentlemen as well. And ask Tobias to put the usual pack together.'

He picked up the two-way radio from its table where it had lain neglected throughout the conversation with Miranda and clipped it to his belt. He refastened his cotton jacket and began to pull on gloves. There was a frown between his brows. He looked alert and preoccupied.

But Miranda could not forget that look of bone-tugging weariness. She said urgently, 'You're exhausted. Can't someone else go?'

His eyes skimmed over her, barely seeming to see her. 'Who did you have in mind? There's no one else here but me who knows the rainforest well enough. That's why the men came here in the first place.'

'Then leave it till morning.'

'By the morning Heitor could be dead,' he said evenly.

Miranda winced. 'At least take someone with you,' she begged. 'You can't have looked in the mirror since you came back. You look terrible.'

He gave a harsh laugh. 'Sorry about that. I'll shave tomorrow.'

'I didn't mean that and you know it,' she said hotly. She went to him and put a hand on his arm. It seemed to her that he stiffened. But he did not shake her off. 'You don't understand. I meant what I said. You're exhausted.'

He said very quietly, 'No. It's you who don't understand. I have to go. Heitor is a friend. Even if he weren't, there is no one but me.'

Miranda said, 'Then take me too.'

She did not know why she said it. The last thing she wanted was to go out into that wild darkness. But somehow she could not bear for Paul to go alone.

He put one hand very gently over her own.

'My dear, it's a kind thought but you don't know what it's like out there.'

Miranda shivered. She looked him in the eye. 'Don't I? Don't forget I was out there with you three nights ago.'

For a moment there was absolute silence in the room. Even the worried villagers were silenced. From his shocked expression it was clear that one of them at least had enough English to understand that last remark. Anna looked from Paul to Miranda and back again. Her pleasant face was full of consternation.

Then, unexpectedly, Paul laughed.

'So you were. How could I have forgotten?' he said ruefully.

'Well, then...'

He shook his head. 'It doesn't turn you into a rainforest survival expert, I'm afraid.' He squeezed her fingers. 'Believe me. I'd just worry about having you with me. Stay here with Anna and make up a room for Heitor. And pray we find him,' he added grimly.

Her fingers clung but he put her hand away from him firmly and turned to the villagers. She recognised that he was not going to change his mind. She blinked away tears. There was no point in making it more difficult for him.

'Be careful,' Miranda said in a voice that shook only slightly.

Paul stiffened. She saw the muscular shoulders go back as if at a blow. He turned back to her. Meeting his eyes, Miranda felt her head suddenly swim.

One hasty step forward and she was in his arms. His mouth was harsh, hurtful. Miranda didn't care. She clung to him, giving him furious kiss for kiss, oblivious of their audience. She was breathless, sobbing a little, when he raised his head.

'I will be back,' he said in a low voice. 'Wait for me.'

'Yes. Oh, yes.'

He let her go, reluctantly, it seemed to her.

'Get some rest. I don't know when I'll be back.' He looked at the housekeeper. 'Make sure she goes to bed, Anna.'

The pleasant face was expressionless. 'Yes, *senhor*.'

'Look after her,' he said softly.

He was gone. The villagers trailed out after him, their expressions thoughtful. Miranda stared at the door as it closed behind them. Her heart was racing. Anna cleared her throat.

'It would be wise,' she said carefully, 'to do as the *patrão* wishes.'

Miranda turned dazed eyes on her. She felt as if she was floating in a golden haze. I'm in love, she thought dreamily.

'I will bring you a hot drink,' the housekeeper promised, a thread of amusement in her voice.

Miranda gave her a blazing smile. Anna blinked. She took the dazzled girl by the elbow.

'Come along,' she said gently. 'You need your rest. You've had a dangerous couple of days.'

Miranda looked at her quickly.

'Dangerous?'

But Anna just smiled enigmatically and urged her upstairs. There Miranda was provided with a hot drink, redolent of exotic fruits and cinnamon, and left to her dreams.

CHAPTER SEVEN

IN THE morning there was news of Paul, though he was not back.

'They found the doctor,' Anna reported. 'The *patrão* radioed Santa Cruz for the helicopter.'

Miranda went cold. 'He's hurt?' she said hoarsely.

Anna shrugged, turning back to the range. 'Am I a doctor?'

'Please. You must tell me. I—need to know.' It was wrung out of her.

Anna gave her a pitying glance. 'The *patrão* is fine. The doctor has hurt his back.'

'Oh,' said Miranda. She felt a slow flush suffuse her whole body. Her eyes fell, ashamed.

Anna said neutrally, 'He will be back as soon as he can. He will have Senhorinha Martins with him.'

'Senhorinha Martins,' Miranda echoed. 'B-but why?'

'Because she was with the doctor when he was hurt, I imagine,' Anna said levelly. She looked down at the vegetables she was preparing and said in an expressionless voice, 'She is an old friend of the *patrão*. A very old friend.'

'Oh,' Miranda said again, but in quite a different tone. She remembered what she had seen herself from the terrace. Was the gorgeous Bebel Paul Branco's mistress, then? She nearly asked Anna but something stopped her. She did not want Anna to tell her, she thought painfully. If it was true she wanted Paul Branco to tell her. And then explain what he had meant by that very public kiss last night. Did he think Miranda was available to entertain him when there was nobody else to hand?

She was seething, she told herself, furious with Paul for his behaviour. She stamped off to the library and tried hard to immerse herself in a book. It did not work. She kept seeing those dark, intent eyes and that look of fire that he had bent on her last night.

She made a discovery. It was not Paul Branco with whom she was furious. It was herself. She felt hurt and humiliated, exposed by that kiss to the ridicule of the entire *fazenda*.

She made another discovery, even more alarming. In spite of her humiliation and anger, she was still desperately concerned for him. Let him be safe, Miranda thought, throwing aside the pre-war novel—and her own sensitivities—without difficulty. *Please* let him be safe.

It turned her cold. Was her foggy delight of last night prophetic, then? Did she feel the same in the cold light of day? Could she really be in love with this enigmatic, arrogant man?

No, thought Miranda. For the first time in years she allowed herself to remember the last few months in the big family house before Harry had brought her out to the Amazon.

Keith Ware had been a friend of the family as long as she could remember. His family were not really rich but they were titled. They inhabited the local stately home. She knew her uncle had been delighted whenever he was asked to shoot over on the estate. It had never occurred to her that at the same time he was setting up an alliance between her cousin Claire and the eldest son. Especially as Keith Ware had sworn he would marry Miranda during a heady session in the car park after a Young Farmers' dance.

She had been very inexperienced, of course, Miranda thought painfully. Even the innocent heroines in Maria Clara's magazines knew more about sex than she did—and the lengths to which it could push otherwise quite civilised people.

Civilised people like Paul Branco? Had last night's kiss been more than a temporary urge, temporarily irresistible? Or did he too, like Lotte, wonder secretly if an innocent partner would be the saving of him? Did he think there was a remote chance that she might save him from that loneliness he had spoken of—and the cynicism that Miranda had seen all too clearly for herself? Was that why he had insisted on her staying at the *fazenda* as firmly as he had insisted on Lotte leaving?

Miranda reviewed their various encounters to date. She sighed. On the evidence so far it seemed unlikely.

The rescued kitten had taken to dividing his time between Miranda's company and the kitchen. Now, finding her stretched out alone on the library's *chaise-longue*, he climbed confidently into her lap. He turned round three times and then curled up with his nose under his paws. She scratched the top of his head absently. He began to purr.

It eased her hurt heart a little. At least with the kitten for company she did not have to pretend that she had her whole attention on the book when the maids came into the room. Half her brain was constantly vigilant, scanning the sounds of the house for indications that its master had returned.

When he did, at last, he was not alone. Bebel Martins was with him. Miranda stood in the doorway of the old stable and felt her heart turn to marble.

It was a moot point which of the two was filthier or more exhausted. Paul looked haggard. But Bebel was a walking zombie. One look at her face and, stone for a heart or no, Miranda flew to put a supporting arm round the slender, swaying figure.

'Thank you,' said Bebel through lips that barely moved. There was a blank look in her eyes. 'I'm sorry,' she said. 'I couldn't go on any more.' Then she collapsed quietly against Miranda's shoulder. Paul took one look at the wilting figure and swept her up into his arms.

'Come with me,' he flung over his shoulder at Miranda.

He carried Bebel to the room she had had before and put her down gently on the bed. Miranda looked at the tall windows and winced. She went across and opened the shutters.

'She's had all she can take,' Paul said soberly, looking down at the still figure on the bed. 'She should never have tried to stick with me.'

Miranda looked at the stark anxiety on his face and felt her heart contract. She fought against the feeling. Bebel Martins needed her help, not misplaced schoolgirl envy. The one thing her mission training had taught her was to help people at the point of exhaustion.

'She needs rest,' she said in a neutral voice. 'She'll be better when she has slept. And she's probably dehydrated. I'll bring her a carafe of water.'

Paul jumped. The look he gave her was almost surprised. As if he had forgotten she was in the room, Miranda thought. She reminded herself, deliberately, that he would be used to being here with Bebel alone. It hurt. She looked away.

He pushed a hand through his hair.

'Yes. You're right, of course.' He hesitated. 'Will you stay with her?'

That hurt even more. Miranda did not allow herself to show it. She turned back and directed her smile carefully at somewhere in the region of his left ear.

'Yes,' she said steadily. 'Of course.'

'Thank you,' he said simply.

He touched the sleeping woman's brow very gently and went out.

Bebel slept heavily for most of the day. Miranda sat with her all the time. Anna sent up cool drinks. From time to time Bebel came back to semi-consciousness and Miranda managed to coax her to drink.

Late in the afternoon she came fully awake and turned her head on the pillow towards Miranda who was standing at the window.

'Heitor?' she said in puzzled voice.

Miranda's eyebrows flew up. Did that mean that Bebel was used to sharing her room with Heitor do Campo as well? Or was it just that she assumed an unknown figure to be that of the doctor? Somehow, from the lazily affectionate tone, Miranda thought it was probably the former. If so, did Paul Branco know? she wondered.

But she went back to the bed and lifted Bebel's wrist. The pulse was reassuringly strong.

'How are you feeling?'

The puzzled look intensified for a moment. Then light dawned. Bebel hauled herself up on the pillows.

'You're Henry Lane's daughter. What...? Oh, I remember.' She put a hand to her head. 'Paul was right, wasn't he? I'm so sorry.'

Miranda stared. 'Paul was right about what?' she said, mystified.

Bebel Martins shook her head. 'I'm not making sense, am I?' she said ruefully. 'I meant about your father. Paul was almost certain he must have died. That's why he wanted to keep you here until the search was complete. He thought it would be easier for you than among a lot of strangers in Santa Cruz.' The beautiful face expressed nothing but warm sympathy. 'I hope he was right?'

So that was why he had insisted on her staying, thought Miranda. Nothing to do with attraction, still less a sense that in her innocence she might be important to him. It was pure pity for the waif of the storm.

She flinched as if the kindly woman on the bed had flung a phial of acid in her face.

'Oh, dear,' said Bebel Martins, seeing the instinctive movement. 'I didn't mean...'

Miranda straightened her shoulders. 'Senhor Branco has been very kind,' she said woodenly.

'And I've been very clumsy.' The woman was remorseful. 'Look, all I meant was I've known Paul Branco a long time and I listen to him.' She gave a little laugh. 'Well, so do most people, I suppose. I let him persuade me that it was right for you to stay here for the time being. But you don't have to. If you have no one in Brazil and no money, you're going to be my professional responsibility anyway. I can arrange for you to leave if that's what you want.'

Miranda flinched. She felt the fury rise again.

'Everyone keeps saying I'm their responsibility. I'm twenty-three, for heaven's sake. Nobody has to take care of me as if I were a child,' she said passionately.

Bebel looked disturbed. 'Of course not. I never...'

'Oh, yes, you did. And so did *he*.' Miranda's voice was filled with sudden loathing. 'Just stop it. Both of you. I can take care of myself.'

She drew a shaky breath. Bebel was looking at her curiously. Miranda thought of her own responsibilities.

'I imagine you'd like a shower or something,' she said stiffly. 'Anna sent up towels. She said you have your own clothes here to change into.'

The woman's eyes were steady. 'Yes.'

Miranda flushed. She did not know why. She already knew the woman was a regular visitor. And she had more than enough evidence of what drew her to the *fazenda*.

She said in a stifled voice, 'Do you need any help?'

'No, thank you.' The voice was cool.

Miranda shrugged. Perhaps she ought to have insisted, she thought. But there was a healthy colour in Bebel's soft cheeks and she really did not want to spend another second in the beautiful Brazilian's company.

'Then I'll see you later downstairs.'

She met one of the maids in the hall.

'The *patrão* wanted to see you, *senhorinha*,' the girl said shyly. 'I told him you were still with Senhorinha Isabel. I'm sorry.'

'I was. I'll go to him now. Where is he?'

'In the office, *senhorinha*.'

Miranda made a face. She had not yet located half the rooms in the sprawling house. 'Where is that?'

The girl smiled. 'Out in the laboratory block. There is a covered way from the stables. I'll show you.'

She did. Miranda followed, her eyebrows climbing. The laboratory block seemed to consist of enormous plant-filled conservatories. But in the end the girl took her to a small white-painted door at the far end of the passage. She knocked perfunctorily and ran off, giggling a little. Which left Miranda to respond alone to the peremptory command to enter.

It was fitted out like a conventional laboratory, at least from what Miranda could recall of school laboratories. Paul himself was seated on a stool peering down a microscope at a piece of fern leaf. He had a tiny computer no bigger than a notebook beside him.

He did not look up.

'You wanted to see me?'

Miranda hated the way she sounded. It was stiff and sulky.

He did look up then. She saw that he had washed and shaved and, presumably, rested. At least, the look of blank exhaustion was gone.

'Yes.'

He nodded at another stool and tapped out a quick note on the machine at his elbow. Miranda watched as he logged off and turned off the power. The gleaming screen darkened.

'What are you doing?' she asked, intrigued.

'Trying to catch up on some long-delayed work.' He put the piece of fern carefully into a small glass container and stowed it in a large refrigerator in the corner of the room.

'Work?'

Paul was amused. 'Did you think I spent my life riding around the rainforest looking for maidens to rescue?'

His eyes were laughing. Miranda flushed, averting her own. Not for the first time in his presence, she felt out of her depth. She tried to remember she was not in love with him.

'Of course not.' She looked round at the glass-fronted cabinets and the workmanlike benches. 'What do you do here?'

'Botanical research.'

The cool answer was so unexpected that she forgot she was avoiding his eyes.

'*Botanical research*?'

He laughed aloud. 'Don't sound so appalled. That's what I am. A botanist. It's why my grandfather left me the *fazenda*.' His mouth compressed suddenly. 'One of the reasons,' he amended. 'We have a small research programme here. Mainly on plants we pick up locally. And those we grow here, of course.'

Miranda shook her head in bewilderment. Orderly academic research was the last thing she would have connected with the arrogant ruffian who had brought her through the rainforest.

'And you run it?' she said dubiously.

'I'm the overall director of the programme, yes.' His eyes danced. 'I'm away too much to be in charge day to day. Rubem runs that side of it.'

That sounded much more likely. 'Away where?' Miranda asked with a touch of scorn.

'Living it up in the low-life bars of Rio,' he said solemnly.

Miranda recognised that she was being teased. She glared at him.

Paul relented. 'I lecture. Mainly for the UN Fund for Nature. Sometimes in universities in Europe or the US. We're looking at endangered species and their properties. I became a hot favourite on the homeopathic circuit for a while,' he added blandly.

Miranda treated that sally with the contempt that it deserved.

'So you only run the jungle rescue service in your spare time?' she challenged, as bland as he.

To her surprise he did not laugh. Instead he shook his head.

'I've never seen anything like the last few days. We'll be lucky if it stays at that, too.'

Abruptly Miranda did not feel like laughing either.

'You mean the storm could come back?'

The handsome face was serious. 'You said yourself the day looked pretty black yesterday. To be honest I was expecting it all last night. I was—concerned about you here alone with just the servants. But Heitor had crushed a couple of ribs. I couldn't leave him.'

More than serious—bleak. He seemed lost in some grim reverie of his own for a moment.

'Expecting what?' Miranda ventured at last.

Paul shook himself. 'The worst,' he said drily. 'It's usually the best policy, I find.'

She winced at the flippancy, the cynicism that grated.

She said more tartly than she intended, 'And what is the worst?'

He regarded her for a long minute, his eyes almost black. Then he said succinctly, 'Hurricane.'

'*Hurricane*? But surely...?'

'You must realise we've been on the edge of something fairly dramatic,' he said in a level tone. 'They haven't got round to calling it a hurricane yet. Perhaps they won't. In theory it has passed, moved on south. In practice——' He shrugged. 'It's not unknown for hurricanes to turn round and come back. We might not be so lucky next time.'

Miranda thought of the drenched and dispossessed refugees who had trailed through the *fazenda's* kitchen, her own gruelling experiences, Paul's look of being at the end of his endurance.

'Lucky?'

'There are still leaves on the trees,' he said evenly. 'The trees are still standing on the whole. Hurricanes don't leave anything behind except a rubbish tip.'

Miranda shivered. 'What are the chances of it coming back?'

'Slight, according to the weather office in Manaus.'

His tone was neutral but Miranda interpreted his true feelings. 'You don't believe them?'

'I don't know. I'm no weather expert. But they're also saying there's no danger of the river rising and they're wrong there. It's up over a metre since this morning. Another couple of metres and it will flood at Rosario.'

'That's serious?'

'The village has been evacuated, so no one should get hurt. But who knows what damage it will do? And the *fazenda* will almost certainly be cut off.' He moved restlessly. 'I ought to get Bebel out of here as soon as possible.' He paused, then added deliberately, 'And you, of course.'

Miranda felt a little stab of panic at the thought of being sent away by the arrogant ruffian. She curbed it.

'Whatever you think best,' she said in a colourless voice.

'I think——' He stopped. 'I think people don't think clearly in the middle of a crisis.'

Miranda bristled. 'If you're saying you're responsible for me again...'

He flung up a hand.

'I'm saying I don't have the right to make myself responsible for you. I'm no white knight and you're—very innocent.'

Miranda glared at him. 'Is that my fault?'

Paul gave a little shaken laugh. 'It's hardly a question of fault. It's just that I—well, I'm not sure that it's a good idea for us to be together too much.'

'Why?' she flung at him.

Briefly he closed his eyes. 'You're not that innocent.'

She took a hasty step forward. 'You mean because you're attracted to me.'

He opened his eyes. 'That's one way of putting it,' he agreed wryly.

'But you're attracted to hundreds of women, aren't you?' Miranda challenged. 'It's no big deal for you. And as for me...' She shrugged. It was very nonchalant. She was very proud of it. 'It had to happen some time.'

A flame leaped into his eyes. Seeing it, Miranda waited pleasurably for him to sweep her up into his arms.

She was completely unprepared for him saying grimly, 'I don't think we'll examine that statement too closely. If I needed an illustration of why you should be moving on fast, there it is.'

Miranda stared at him. 'I don't understand.'

'Don't you?' She could see that he was furious. 'Bebel was right. God preserve me from sweet young innocents.'

Miranda had never felt so humiliated in her life.

'I am not a sweet young innocent,' she shouted at him.

'Oh, yes, you are.'

Paul did not raise his voice but the effect of his words was like a whip. Miranda winced away from it. He looked volcanic. And then he did sweep her up into his arms.

It was a totally adult kiss. She felt scorched by the merciless passion of it—scorched and suddenly, terribly afraid. When he let her go she was on the edge of tears. He looked at her grimly.

'And heaven help me that's how you're going to leave here. Preferably as soon as possible.'

She retreated. 'I hate you!' Her voice shook.

'Good,' Paul said coolly. 'Work on it. It's the best insurance either of us is likely to find. Now get out of here while I finish my work.'

Miranda was speechless. He pulled the little computer towards him and flicked on the power switch. With an exclamation Miranda whirled and fled out of the laboratory.

It did not help to find Bebel Martins sitting in the drawing-room, leafing through an American fashion magazine. She looked like something out of the magazine herself, Miranda thought, trying to be generous. Her loose navy jacket over matching trousers and dazzling white blouse made her look like the international fashion world's idea of a sailor. In her borrowed Edwardiana,

Miranda felt like a child dressed up in its elder sister's clothes by comparison.

Bebel looked up with an unshadowed smile.

'Hi.'

'Hello,' said Miranda and added conscientiously, 'How do you feel now?'

'Human again. There was a point this morning when I thought I'd turned into a tree frog,' Bebel said wryly. 'That was my first and last experience under canvas in the forest. And you managed a whole night of it. I must say I don't envy you.'

Miranda was disarmed. 'It was certainly memorable,' she agreed.

She remembered the feel of Paul's long body against hers in the darkness of the tent and shivered suddenly. 'I wouldn't want to do it again.'

But even as she said it she knew it wasn't true. Bebel Martins smiled and began to discuss the clothes in her magazine. Miranda listened with half an ear.

Oh, no, it wasn't true at all. She would do anything, go through anything, to be close to Paul Branco again. He had patronised and rejected her. Yet, she thought, appalled, it made no difference. Just the thought of that taut, handsome face and her bones melted. Her blood turned to honey in her veins and all she wanted was to hold him close and love him.

Love. Yes, that was it. It was not adolescent lust. It was not even her inexperience. She had met Rolf, the young anthropologist, when she was younger and more impressionable than she was now. No, inexperienced she might be but she had lived with absolute values for long enough to recognise one. This was love.

Miranda sat down rather suddenly. She felt dazed. And rather alarmed. It was one thing to feel you were in love with a man who held you and seemed to care for you. It was quite another to realise that you still loved a man who had just been berating you. Especially, she thought drily, when you subsequently found yourself in the sole company of the woman who was almost certainly his mistress.

Miranda was cruelly torn. Half of her hugged the new awareness to her with a sort of shy pride. At the same time she felt the hopelessness of it. Paul himself had already warned her, she remembered.

'Are you all right?' she heard Bebel ask. It seemed to come from a very long way off.

'What?' She looked up and saw her companion put aside her magazine, looking concerned. 'Oh, yes, perfectly. I—er—I just remembered something.'

'Nothing pleasant from the looks of it.'

Pleasant? Miranda smiled privately. It was heaven and hell and deeply alarming. But no, it wasn't pleasant.

'If you ever want to talk...' Bebel began gently.

Miranda's eyes filled with sudden tears. What could she say? I am in love with the man you sometimes sleep with? She shook her head.

Bebel sighed. But she let the subject drop, to Miranda's great relief. In fact the Brazilian woman seemed altogether preoccupied. Even when Paul joined them and they sat down to dinner, Bebel did not lose her abstracted air.

It was not an easy meal. Paul was at his most remote. Miranda, all too conscious of their earlier exchange, was tongue-tied.

But there was nothing the matter with her powers of observation. Watching Paul and Bebel together, she confirmed her hunch that there was no question of love between them. They liked each other. They were pleasant to each other. At some moments during that interminable dinner, Miranda wondered if they even realised the other was there.

Somehow, it seemed to make the whole thing worse. If she could have told herself that Paul was in love with Bebel, it would have hurt but there would not be this unendurable sense of waste.

Miranda drank wine, which she was unaccustomed to, picked at her food and retreated into monosyllables. She barely raised her head when Paul got to his feet.

'I'll just finish my notes,' he said. 'I'll take my coffee into the study.'

'Of course.' Bebel seemed to focus on him with an effort. 'I'll see you later?'

Miranda averted her eyes. She could feel Paul watching her but there was nothing she could do to disguise her expression.

'Of course,' he said coolly.

When he had gone silence fell. Bebel played with a tiny silver apostle spoon. She was frowning. It looked as if she was wrestling with a knotty problem.

At last she raised her head. 'I'm not being much company, am I?' she said ruefully. 'I'm sorry. Put it down to the jungle. I was very scared out there.'

Miranda sympathised in spite of herself.

'Perhaps you ought to go to bed,' she said gruffly. 'Rest is the best thing.'

Bebel nodded wearily. 'I'm sure you're right. I'll leave you, then. Goodnight.'

'Goodnight,' said Miranda.

Left alone in the dining-room, she felt the room's shadows press in on her. How long before Paul joined Bebel Martins in that room upstairs? she thought, torturing herself. He might not love her but he was a virile, sophisticated man and she was beautiful.

He had got used to settling for emotional second-best, Miranda thought. That was why he was so cynical. Sometimes he forgot to mock and then you saw the real man.

What would it take to bring out the real man? Miranda wondered, trembling. If you loved him. If you could forget that scorching hand-grenade of a kiss. Maybe Lotte had been right. Maybe he needed someone to give without counting the cost. She swallowed. Did she *dare*?

Paul's study was unknown territory. It was on a different level from the main house. The wing was in darkness except for a thin light round the edge of the heavily carved door. Miranda pushed it open and eased inside.

It was a plain room, plainer than any other she had seen in this house of luxury. There were maps on the walls and a scatter of brilliant native rugs on the floor. And everywhere there were books. Books in the carved shelves, books on the carved and curlicued tables, books on the floor. Like him, it had no softness anywhere. She walked forward.

Paul hadn't noticed her approach. He had a glass in his hand. His booted feet rested on the antique desk in front of him. His dark head was bent and he was watching the golden liquid as he swirled it round and round. He had discarded the jacket he had worn at dinner and was in his shirt-sleeves. The shirt was unbuttoned, throwing the dark column of his throat into dramatic relief against the whiteness. In the sharp shadows cast by the desk lamp, his face looked appallingly grim.

Miranda looked at him with misgiving. Her resolution wobbled. She took a hesitant step towards him.

He looked up then, sharply, as if he was braced for an enemy. His eyebrows twitched together when he saw her.

'What are you doing here?' Neither the words nor the tone was welcoming.

Miranda drew a deep breath. 'I thought you might...' Meeting the dark gaze, she abruptly forgot what she was going to say.

His eyes narrowed in a frown. 'Might what, Miranda?'

'Want some company,' she said at last. It sounded lame even to her.

The dark eyes did not flicker. They were fixed on her face. So why did she feel he wasn't seeing her? She changed to her left foot.

'It seemed a shame for us each to be having coffee on our own,' Miranda floundered on.

'So you decided to be sociable?'

There was nothing in the innocent tone of enquiry to bring the blood storming into her cheeks, Miranda thought, furious with herself.

'Er—yes.'

'Thoughtful of you.'

Miranda bit her lip. She hadn't realised it would be so difficult.

'So I'll ring for coffee, shall I?' she asked.

His smile glinted. It must be a trick of the light that made it look so devilish.

'Oh, I think that would be a waste, don't you?'

'What?'

'You don't like my coffee,' he reminded her gently. 'And I am well-supplied with such stimulants as I need.'

She stared. He raised the glass in his hand.

'Whisky,' he said. 'Try some.'

The sharp aromatic scent of the alcohol was strong. Miranda shook her head in revulsion. He gave a slow smile that made him look wicked.

'Come on, missionary's daughter. If you're going to convert me, you'll have to do better than that.'

Miranda jumped. 'Convert you?'

He shrugged. 'Isn't that why you're down here? I had the impression this afternoon that you'd had enough of my company to last you a lifetime.'

Miranda felt as if she'd been stripped. Her eyes fell before his cynical expression.

He relented a little. 'You haven't been at the salvation game very long, have you, Miranda? When you have you'll find out it's just as much a series of bargains as everything else in this world. So much virtue on earth for so much reward in heaven. And sometimes the seller pushes the price up.'

Her eyes lifted. He bewildered her. His mouth quirked. He looked grim but when he spoke his voice was almost gentle.

'I'm not bargaining, Miranda. I don't know whether this is your own idea or whether the German woman put you up to it...'

She flushed, instantly and undisguisably.

'Ah. So that's it.'

He brought his feet down from the desk with a thump. He got lazily to his feet.

'Well, I know what Lotte Meyer wants—another mission upcountry. I've already told her—she won't get it. Which brings us to you. What do *you* think you're doing here at this time of night offering prettily to take coffee with me? What are you really after, Miranda?'

She met the dark eyes and found she couldn't lie.

'I don't want you to go to Bebel Martins tonight,' she blurted.

CHAPTER EIGHT

PAUL went as still as if she had shot him. There was a shivery silence.

'Don't you, by God?' he said at last, very softly.

He strolled across to her. 'And why is that, Miranda?'

His eyes were mocking. Miranda looked away, flushing.

'Don't go to her,' she said rapidly, stumbling over the words. She thought of the abstraction she had seen in Bebel, the frowning remoteness in him. 'You don't care about her, not really, and she doesn't love you.'

'True.'

The soft word stopped her dead. Her eyes flew to his face. Was he angry? But his expression was one of cool amusement, nothing more. When he saw her trepidation he laughed aloud.

'Of course it's true, my sweet Miranda. If either of us had thought there was any question of love we would have put the world between us before we got involved.'

'But—I thought—aren't you—er—in love with Senhorinha Martins?' she stammered.

'You said I didn't really care for her,' Paul reminded her.

'I meant truly, if you examined your heart, that it was a shallow sort of feeling,' Miranda said earnestly.

Just for an instant something flashed in his eyes. She took a step backwards before she realised she had done so. Then he was laughing again.

'And what do you know of feelings, shallow or otherwise, missionary's daughter?' he mocked.

That hurt. But Miranda was no coward. She lifted her chin.

'I know that love is stronger than anything,' she said quietly.

His face darkened. 'Love,' he said contemptuously. 'And what do you think you mean by that poor, misused word?'

She met his eyes levelly. 'Not whatever it is that you and Senhorinha Martins have for each other,' she told him, suddenly angry. How dared he patronise her like that? How *dared* he?

Paul gave a soft laugh. She had the impression that he was very angry. 'Well, you've learned something in this house at any rate. Bebel and I understand each other.' He paused and then added deliberately, watching her out of narrowed eyes, 'It suits us both very well.'

Miranda winced and tried to school her expression. Not with a great deal of success.

'Don't look like that,' he said, flicking her chin with one long forefinger. 'It isn't for you to approve or disapprove. You're my guest, not my conscience.'

'I wasn't...'

'Yes, you were. I put it down to bad early training,' he said wickedly. 'Only in your case it was training to set yourself up as everybody else's judge.'

Miranda was horrified. 'I don't.'

'Don't you?' His mouth slanted. 'Then why am I not to go to Bebel tonight?'

Which of course was impossible to answer. She hesitated. But her courage failed her. She could not tell him about her own newly recognised love for him. She *could not*. As he said himself, he was not kind. He would laugh at her. She could not face that.

Her eyes fell. To her fury she could feel herself flushing again.

'Silence? No gospel of love to turn me from my evil ways?' Paul prompted maliciously.

She made a helpless gesture.

'You don't understand.'

'Don't I? Well, you're the missionary's daughter. Enlighten me. What is this poor thing called love, in your estimation?'

The sarcasm bit. Miranda gathered her forces together without much hope.

'Love is when you want the good of another person more than you care about your own,' she said at last in a low voice. 'When you'll give up all the trivial things, like your dignity, your pride, for that one important thing.'

There was a little silence. Paul turned away sharply with an angry movement.

'That sounds like a bad case of martyrdom. To say nothing of moral superiority. Deeply suspect,' he said with irony. 'And there's still a bargain there, you notice. You may not want to admit it, but it's there all right. You sacrifice your pride and dignity for this mythical other person—and then he's supposed to sacrifice himself right back, isn't he?'

Miranda shook her head. 'I said you wouldn't understand.'

'Oh, I understand all right.' His voice was hard. 'We're into the realms of fairy-story here. What did Lotte say to you to send you down here like this, Miranda? The wicked man saved by the love of a good woman?'

Miranda stared. It struck a horrid chord. Lotte had only hinted, of course. But it had made an impact because it was a scenario she had already been half contemplating herself. Inspired by Maria Clara's magazine stories, no doubt, she thought, despising herself. She pressed her hands to her hot cheeks.

Paul laughed softly. It wasn't a pleasant laugh. He reached out a long arm and touched her face. It was a gentle touch. It was also almost contemptuous.

'The deal here is that I can have you if I give up Bebel and let Lotte preach at the new medical centre. Isn't it?'

'No,' said Miranda, horrified, as much at her own thoughts as at what he was saying.

'Oh, I know we dress it up differently.' Paul sounded savage under the light sarcasm. 'You love me. I love you. We both love the world. But that's the bargain under the fancy dress. It's a game. Face it.'

She lifted her head. 'I don't play games with love,' she told him.

He shrugged. 'We all play games with love. We can't avoid it. It's in the chemistry.'

'I don't believe that.'

He looked at her consideringly for a moment. 'You really are dangerously naïve,' he said at last. 'Of course, you've had a total-immersion course in self-deception. I mustn't forget that.'

Miranda shook her head. 'No, I'm not deceiving myself.'

'I assure you you are.' His voice had an edge to it.

She gave a soft laugh. 'Love means more than a bargain to me. More than a game. We just have a different view of it.'

'You don't know what you're talking about,' Paul said irritably.

Miranda thought of her carefully secret love. Her smile was sad.

'I assure you I do,' she mocked gently.

He swung round in one of his quick, elegant movements and came close. He turned her face up to his, looking at her searchingly. Miranda withstood it with what composure she could manage. Eventually he gave an impatient sigh.

'You're a child.'

His hand fell. Miranda caught it fiercely.

'I'm not.'

The long, elegant fingers flinched, almost as if they'd been burned. She hardly noticed, in her intensity.

'Believe me. I *know* love isn't about bargains,' she asserted.

For a long moment he looked down at her, his face unreadable. The beautiful hand turned in hers and took a masterful grip of her own. He looked as if he'd come to a decision.

'You're going to tell me all about love, are you, little one?' he said with a softness that even Miranda realised was dangerous.

But she went on bravely, 'Love is giving, not making deals,' and as the sardonic expression didn't change she said, 'Oh, if only I could show you how wrong you are.'

His eyes narrowed at her passionate tone. There was a silence full of their unexpressed trial of strength.

'Maybe you can,' Paul told her, at last.

It was the last thing she was expecting. And yet it didn't sound like the concession it was supposed to be. For some reason, Miranda tensed.

He said in that soft, reasonable tone she had come to dread, 'My experience tells me that women never do anything without a motive. Most of all when they're talking about love. On the other hand, as a woman you are quite out of my experience.'

It was a challenge. Miranda stiffened, freezing into immobility. Unexpectedly, he took their clasped hands to his mouth and held the softness of her inner palm against his lips. He never took his eyes off her face. She shivered.

'Disinterested love,' he mused. 'It's an attractive idea. Giving everything for the greater good of another. Would you do that, Miranda? Give everything?'

She nodded. Her pulses were driving like the storm rain. He kissed her palm lingeringly. She swallowed.

'For me?'

She suddenly realised where this was taking her. She shut her eyes tight and nodded again. I must be crazy, she thought.

'No promises,' he warned her. 'No exclusive rights. No deal for tomorrow. Nothing but purest love.' His voice was cynical.

Miranda hesitated. She opened her eyes cautiously and found him looking at her with an odd expression—half-triumph, half something darker. Her eyes widened.

'You see. You don't like it any more than any other sensible person,' he said drily. 'When you give you want to take in return. As I said, love is a bargain.'

He dropped her hand and turned away.

Miranda said in a voice she didn't recognise, 'I'll prove it isn't.'

Paul stopped dead. He stared straight ahead, as if he was concentrating on blotting her out of his consciousness, Miranda thought suddenly. She went to him and put her hand on the bare bronzed skin under the open shirt. He tensed.

'That's what you want, isn't it?' she said gently.

He said her name on a shaken underbreath.

'I know,' Miranda whispered. She was shaking uncontrollably. 'You want me to step out of my comfortable conventions and not ask for any insurance. You've wanted that since the day I came here, haven't you?'

His hand went to cover hers where it lay on his chest.

'You're not as naïve as you look,' he said without expression.

'Put that down to the education of this house, too,' Miranda said. 'It wouldn't have occurred to me a week ago. You've taught me a lot, Paul Branco.'

'None of which you wanted to learn,' he pointed out. He almost flung her away from him. 'This is ridiculous. You don't know what you're doing. Go back to Lotte, little one.' He was buttoning his shirt with quick, impatient movements. 'You'll be safe up there.'

Miranda said, 'We weren't talking about safety. We were talking about love.'

'You were talking about love,' Paul corrected her swiftly. 'I was talking about real life.'

'They're the same.'

He turned on her suddenly. The handsome face was unreadable but his eyes were glittering like a duellist's.

'Real life,' he said, 'is about hunger and need and learning to live without the means to satisfy either.' He took her by the shoulders. 'Grow up, Miranda. The sort of love you're talking about doesn't exist outside grand opera. In real life people give what they can afford in order to get back what they can use.'

Ignoring the punishing grip on her shoulders, she took his face between her hands.

'Let me prove it. Give me a chance,' she whispered.

He took a sharp step back from her. 'You're living in a fairy-tale,' he said. He sounded coldly despairing.

The coldness frightened her more than his anger or his cynicism. She began to see that this was indeed her only chance to convince him.

She took his hand in a clumsy, unpractised movement and pressed it to her breast.

'Is it a fairy-tale that you want me?' she demanded, seeing his reaction.

He froze. For a moment he seemed to stop breathing. Then, 'No. But wanting is different. I've wanted many women,' he told her brutally. His voice softened a little. 'You think you want me now. But you haven't seen many men in the last five years. There will be plenty of others.'

'But you want me. Now. Don't you?' she challenged him.

Their eyes met; locked. The handsome mouth twisted as if he was in pain.

'Yes.'

She felt a little surge of triumph.

'And you would take me if you thought there wasn't a hidden bargain. If you didn't think you were going to have to pay for it in some obscure way.'

He brushed it aside. 'There always is...'

'No,' said Miranda quietly.

She began to undo her silky blouse. Her fingers shook a little. She pushed the material aside and pressed his hand against her burning skin. She stared into his eyes.

'No price. No bargain. No reproaches,' she said.

Paul stood like stone. Miranda searched his face. She didn't doubt that he wanted her, even if he didn't love her. Why wasn't he making love to her? He had gone readily enough into the arms of Bebel Martins.

Miranda drew a shaky breath. She caressed the back of his hand with gentle fingertips.

'You're playing with fire.' The chiselled lips barely moved.

'I told you. I don't play games with love,' she murmured, still stroking.

'This is not love,' he said harshly.

But Miranda had gone beyond the ability to argue. He was too clever; she could never win an argument with him anyway. She was trembling deeply. She bent her head swiftly and touched her mouth to the hand at her breast. His indrawn breath sounded like a thunderclap in the silence.

'Seduction, Miranda?' But there was a note in the cool, dispassionate voice she had never heard before.

She reached up to his mouth blindly. He took her by the shoulders and held her away from him. His hands bit into the tender flesh like a vice. But they weren't entirely steady.

'You don't think I've got any scruples at all, do you?'

He was rejecting her. In spite of the fact that he said he wanted her—that she *knew* he wanted her—he was going to send her away. She couldn't believe it. A feeling she didn't recognise took hold of her, part panic, part urgency. If she let him turn her away now, they would be strangers and enemies for the rest of their lives, she thought dimly. She couldn't bear it.

She bent her head and touched her mouth, very tenderly, to the back of the hand on her shoulder.

An expletive tore out of him. Then he was holding her, crushing her. He had not crushed Bebel, Miranda thought exultantly, not that evening nor when she had seen them together in Bebel's room. His mouth was hungry.

She had been right, Miranda thought, surrendering to glorious sensation. There was no doubt that Paul Branco wanted her.

And then, as he lifted her from the floor and looked down into her wide green eyes, he said the one thing, the only thing, that could have dispelled the glory.

'Before this goes any further, I think it's only fair to warn you, Miranda. I don't make promises. In bed or out of it.'

There was a tiny silence. Paul looked down at her mockingly. But behind the mockery there was something else.

'Put me down,' Miranda said breathlessly.

He laughed down into her face. 'You're sure? After all that trembling passion, too. You're very convincing, you know. For a girl of limited experience.'

She flushed but said steadily, 'Put me down, please.'

'Second thoughts about surrendering your all for no return?'

Miranda winced. 'It's not a bargain for me. I told you. But I can't—pretend not to know that is exactly what it is for you. I may have limited experience but I am not entirely a fool. Put me down, please.'

With an exaggerated care that was an insult in itself, Paul lowered her to her feet. The hunger of a moment ago had been completely banished from his expression. Now he looked tough, cynical and faintly bored.

'Very wise.' He turned back to his desk. 'I suggest you write to Lotte and tell her you did your best and it didn't work. Bebel will deliver it for you.'

Miranda flinched from the cool sarcasm—and the deliberate reference to Bebel Martins. It hurt but it was a matter of pride not to let him see how much.

'You're wrong. It had nothing to do with Lotte,' she said quietly. She half turned away. 'I'm going to bed.'

He shrugged. 'In the circumstances, I shall take it that that is not an invitation,' he said cynically.

Miranda folded her lips together to stop herself crying out in protest. She hesitated, searching his face.

'What has made you like this?' she said slowly. 'So—distrustful.'

His eyebrows rose. 'It's called growing up.'

Miranda's chin lifted at that. 'I'm twenty-three,' she reminded him between clenched teeth.

'No one would credit it. Your education could do with a great deal of improvement,' he told her brutally.

The green eyes sparked. 'It seems I'm getting it, doesn't it?' she retorted with spurious sweetness.

She thought there was a reluctant glimmer of respect in the dark eyes. 'Not before time,' he said. But he no longer sounded cruel. He sounded infinitely weary instead. 'Oh, go to bed, my child. Before you grow up more than either of us is prepared for.'

She did.

The respect helped. Otherwise she would have felt utterly humiliated, Miranda thought, huddling the kitten to her back in her own room. She did not think she had ever made such a fool of herself in her life. She would never, she promised herself, do so again.

And she would do her best never to set eyes on Paul Branco again either. In spite of the problems with Keith and Claire, she would have to write to Uncle Neil. She would ask Bebel Martins to help her arrange her departure from the Fazenda Branco as well.

In the meantime she would avoid Paul, she vowed. Even if it meant that she had to hide in broom cupboards while he went past.

Yet, when Bebel Martins sat down to breakfast the next morning and said, 'Are you coming back to Santa Cruz with me in the helicopter?' Miranda shook her head vigorously.

'Not today. Not yet. I'm not ready.'

Bebel looked perturbed. Miranda wondered suddenly whether Paul had discussed their encounter last night. She winced at the thought.

'I know it's difficult, my dear. But you'll have to face civilisation again one day. Is there anything to be gained by putting it off?'

Miranda sent up a silent prayer of thanks that Bebel had found such an easy reason for her reluctance to leave the Fazenda Branco.

'I need time,' she muttered.

Bebel sighed. 'You may be right. But——'

Miranda lifted her head. 'But?'

'Is it really wise staying here with Paul on your own?' Bebel asked gently.

Miranda's mouth set. 'That's what Lotte Meyer said.'

Bebel look momentarily annoyed. 'That woman! I wasn't talking about the gossip, my dear. Not even the conventions. It's you I'm thinking of. He's very attractive and—— Oh, you know what I'm going to say. You've led such a sheltered life. He could hurt you badly. Of course, you're different from most young women of your age,' she ended doubtfully.

Not that different, Miranda thought with irony. She did not say anything.

Bebel sighed again. 'I *told* Paul——' She bit it off abruptly. 'Well, I'd better go and see whether Rubem has talked the rescue service into letting me hitch a lift,' she added in some disarray. 'If you're sure you don't want to come too?'

Miranda shook her head.

'Well, you know your own business best,' Bebel said unconvincingly.

The helicopter touched down to take her back several hours later. In all that time, Miranda had not seen Paul. He emerged from his office with an arm round Bebel when the noise of the helicopter made itself heard. He took her to the machine, and had a few words with the pilot, before stepping back. It did not seem an emotional farewell, thought Miranda, watching painfully for signs of physical closeness.

It was not like the last time he and Miranda had seen off the helicopter. This time there was no friendly conversation. Instead he ran lightly past her, with barely an acknowledgement of her presence. Miranda stared after him, half affronted, half cut to the quick.

She masked the hurt quickly. There was no point in letting him see he could give her pain, after all. At best it would give him an excuse to send her back to Santa Cruz. At worst, he could use it as evidence that she was the vulnerable, immature creature he seemed to want to think she was.

So she squared her shoulders and followed him indoors impassively.

She found that he had gone immediately to the kitchen. He was talking crisply to the assembled household.

'The water is already up to one point eight metres. The dam at Rosario looked shaky last night. The pilot tells me they are pulling the emergency services out. That means they think there's at least a chance that it will blow,' she heard him say. He looked round at the solemn-faced maids, Anna and an anxious Rubem. 'I don't have to tell you how serious that is. We could be marooned here for God knows how long. The water supply will almost certainly be contaminated. We have enough oil and bottled gas to keep going for ten days, I reckon. Anyone who wants to make a run for their home must go now.'

There was a murmur.

'The pilot was very clear he won't be back. The emergency is getting worse. We've got food and a roof over our heads, after all. So there won't be another airlift into Santa Cruz—unless someone breaks a leg,' he added grimly. 'But if you want to be with your families and you have to cross the river, you should go now.'

The maids looked from one to the other. After some hesitation it was clear that they all wanted to go. Even Anna, Miranda realised with surprise. It had never occurred to her that Anna did not normally live at the *fazenda*.

Paul nodded. 'I'll get the four-wheel drive,' he said briskly. 'I can take you as far as the ford.'

Rubem said, 'Paul...'

Paul looked round. 'But you live here——' he began. Then he stopped, 'Oh, you want to be with Elena, of course,' he said.

Rubem looked conscience-stricken. 'But the plants...'

'People are more important than plants,' Paul said wryly. 'I've no doubt I'll manage to look after them myself for a few days. Go, Rubem. It will mean I don't have to go to the ford and come back. You can take the truck and stay in the village.' He looked round. 'Come along. Five minutes to collect your belongings. You need to move *fast*, or the ford will be too high to cross.'

They moved then, like a whirlwind called up by his words. Miranda stepped rapidly away from the door as Anna Santos flashed past her, moving at a speed that belied her bulk.

Paul tossed the keys of the truck to Rubem.

'Drive like hell,' he recommended softly.

The man caught the keys deftly, grinned agreement and ran. Miranda heard high voices, some laughing, and then the unmistakable noise of the big vehicle's engine.

As the sound slowly faded, Paul's shoulders seemed to lower with relief. He met her eyes across the kitchen. For the first time in an age, it seemed to Miranda, he smiled at her.

'Alone at last,' he said drily.

Miranda caught her breath. The coldness he had shown earlier had dropped away like a cloak he no longer needed. He seemed to have forgotten that he had called her a child. The dark, amused eyes were not looking at her as if she were a child, she thought with a little shiver that was pure excitement.

'Yes.' Her voice was a breathless whisper.

He did not move towards her. 'Are you afraid?'

'Of the river rising?' She shook her head. 'No.'

Though if he meant was she afraid of him she would not be able to answer so unequivocally, Miranda thought. But it was a delicious sort of trepidation, not real fear.

'Are you?' she asked curiously.

He considered it. 'I've been in bad storms. Even a hurricane once. Given a choice, I'd rather avoid it. But if we're sensible we won't get hurt.'

He turned to the big sink and lowered the plug. Then he began to fill it.

'Fill everything you can find with water,' he instructed over his shoulder. 'That will be the worst shortage. Fill all the baths and basins. Any bowls you can find, too.'

She did. They worked hard until the sullen afternoon light was gone. Then Paul switched on the light.

'We'll have to be careful with electricity,' he said. 'The generator gobbles oil.'

'Have you got oil lamps?' Miranda asked practically.

The fine brows rose. 'A practical thought. Yes, we have somewhere. Though I'm damned if I know how they work.'

'I do,' Miranda said with composure. Henry Lane's mission had not possessed its own generator.

'Then come with me.'

He found the lamps. It took a longer search to find the paraffin oil on which they ran but Miranda eventually identified it at the back of a broom cupboard. Triumphant, she bore their trove into the kitchen.

'The wicks need trimming,' she said, setting about it, 'and they're dusty. But apart from that they're perfectly all right.'

Paul swung round a kitchen chair and sat astride it, watching her with appreciative amusement.

'You never cease to surprise me,' he remarked.

Miranda looked up from her task enquiringly. 'Because I know how to light an oil lamp?'

'Because you seem so fragile at one point and then all of a sudden you turn hugely competent.'

Miranda laughed. She polished dust off the copper base of the lamp with a handful of skirt.

'I'm not fragile. You just think I am.'

'Not just me,' he said slowly. 'Bebel was reminding me how—young—you are.'

Miranda made a rude noise. 'Twenty-three is hardly in the schoolroom.'

'Maybe not, but you have to admit you've led a rather eccentric life these last few years,' Paul said drily.

She looked at him over the top of the lamps. 'And you haven't?' she said with composure.

At his look of astonishment she laughed aloud.

'It's just a different sort of eccentricity, that's all.'

The dark eyes gleamed. 'So you think we're both peculiar? Both different from the herd? We've just chosen different ways to make our point?

Miranda breathed on the brass of another lamp and rubbed it till it shone. 'Yes.'

He folded his arms along the back of the chair and rested his chin on them. He needed a shave again, Miranda thought. Dusty from his explorations, he looked like a pirate. It made something clench hard in her stomach. She concentrated hard on the sixty-year-old lamp before her. She might be in love with him but there was no point in making him a present of the knowledge. She had a feeling she was going to need all the advantages she could get in the next few days.

'So you think we're alike?' Paul Branco said thoughtfully.

Miranda allowed herself a little gentle irony. 'Not in everything, perhaps.'

He laughed. He stood up. She was almost certain he was coming towards her when there was a tremendous crash. It was too reminiscent of those scary hours while she'd sat in the mission house, trying to nerve herself to leave. She went white.

Paul saw it at once. 'Sure you're not scared?'

'N-no.'

'You don't have to be brave, you know. It's perfectly acceptable to be scared. It's mostly noise at the moment, though.'

Miranda shivered at the implication that it would be worse when it was more than only noise.

Paul took a decision. 'Let's see if those things work and then we can take them into the drawing-room and have a drink by the flickering light of my grandmother's lamps. How's that for a romantic prospect?'

Miranda stood up. She was grateful for the change of subject. 'Of course they'll work,' she said, affronted. 'And they don't flicker either. They're perfectly all right to read by.'

He took two from her and smiled down at her with that warmth that set her heart beating, no matter what they were talking about.

'But I don't want to read. I want a civilised evening in my own drawing-room. We can have a drink and talk about the state of the Union. Tell our life histories.'

Miranda gave a slightly tremulous laugh. 'You don't need to go that far. I'm not going to throw a scene.'

Paul backed through the kitchen door and held it open with his body for her to pass him.

'No, you aren't, are you?' he said in a meditative tone.

They went into the darkened drawing-room. The shutters had been locked and bolted in here as they had in the rest of the house. Miranda shivered as the shutters rattled. It sounded like outlaws hammering for admittance, she thought: violent and somehow angry.

In the shadows Paul set down the lamps he was carrying and pulled a lighter from his pocket. Miranda heard the little mechanical click and hiss followed by a tiny flare. He applied it to a wick. In the stark chiaroscuro, Miranda saw that his hand did not shake even the slightest.

'You're not a bit afraid, are you?' she said, impressed and reassured.

'I've learned to deal with the elements.' His voice was dry. 'There are other things to be afraid of in my case.'

Miranda curled up on the end of the *chaise-longue*.

'The story of our lives?' she murmured mischievously.

There was an oddly charged silence.

Then he said, 'I think not,' almost curtly.

'Oh,' said Miranda, surprised and a little offended. 'I didn't mean your *secrets*...'

He strode over and sat down beside her on the *chaise-longue*. She moved her feet to give him room. It left a small but important space between them. He gave her a dry look.

'Secrets aren't the problem, Miranda,' he said. 'It's what's behind the secrets. Things you want, things you feel, things you won't admit to, even to yourself. It's not good, repressing emotions,' he said deliberately.

Miranda stared at him. 'I'm not repressing my emotions.'

In the light of the distant lamp she thought she saw his eyes flicker. Then he leaned away from her, his arms along the back of the seat.

'Oh, but you are.' His tone was teasing again. 'If you're afraid you should express it. Scream. Rave at me for bringing you here in the first place. Hit me if you want.' He smiled suddenly. 'Let it out and you get rid of it. Push it down inside you and you're just building up problems for the future.'

In spite of the casual tone, the dark eyes were surprisingly penetrating. Quite kind, Miranda thought, meeting them uneasily. But they saw too much.

A sudden heat invaded her. She did not quite understand it. But she knew she was suddenly alarmed at how much those eyes might see of her feelings...her unacknowledged love.

Miranda said carefully, 'But maybe one will be better able to deal with the problems in the future. Perhaps postponing them is a good idea. If you can't deal with them now, I mean.'

There was another sizzling silence.

'You could handle a good scream,' Paul said at last, amused.

So he had not seen so much. Perversely, Miranda found she wanted him to see more. She smiled, but absently.

'Maybe. But there are a lot of things I couldn't handle just now,' she said.

It invited his questioning. It was deeply dangerous. She held her breath. Another, longer silence. Miranda felt as if he was willing her to speak. But she did not. She could not.

Then Paul said in a husky voice, 'I know. You don't have to tell me. Why do you think I——?'

He broke off, scanning her tense face. His eyes darkened. He said something under his breath. Miranda thought it sounded suspiciously like swearing. He stood up and made a great show of adjusting the wick of the lamp.

'Don't try to be too well-behaved, Miranda,' he said over his shoulder. 'You've had a rough time.' He paused. 'I don't just mean during the storm, either. You're entitled to make a fuss if you want to.'

She watched him painfully. And he would comfort her, as he had on the day of the floods? As if she were a child? Couldn't he see that she didn't want that? She didn't think she could bear it if he called her a child again.

She said, 'Don't be kind to me, Paul.'

He stood very still, his back to her. Then he made a quick repudiating gesture, as if the idea disgusted him.

'I'm the last man in the world to be kind to anyone. You know that. It isn't being kind to tell a lonely adolescent she has a right to her feelings.'

Miranda felt as if he had hit her. 'A lonely adolescent'.

'Is that how you see me?' she whispered.

He did not look at her. 'It doesn't take great insight,' he said drily. 'How could you not be lonely in the mission, with only a half mad father for company?'

'There were the people who came to school. And the children,' Miranda said with an effort.

She could not bear his pity. She *could* not.

He turned then. Even in the deeply shadowed room she could see that his eyes were compassionate.

'And they all went away again about their own affairs,' he said gently. 'You don't have to pretend to me, Miranda. You told me about your loneliness. I know that feeling well enough, God help me.' The handsome mouth twisted. 'Another thing in which we're alike.'

She protested, 'I don't think...'

Paul strode across to her and went down on his haunches in front of her. His eyes were piercing.

'Don't you?' he said in a steely voice. It was an accusation.

Miranda drew back.

'Isn't that exactly what you think?' Paul insisted. 'That we're a couple of outcasts anyway so what have we got to lose?'

She swallowed. 'I don't know what you mean.'

'Oh, but I think you do.' He was at his softest, deadliest. 'You're far too intelligent not to. Inexperienced, yes, a fool, no. God help me, never a fool.'

Miranda searched his face. She could see that he was angry, blindingly angry. It was all the more alarming for the iron control he was imposing on it. And somehow it seemed to be her fault.

She moistened her dry lips again. He was so close that she could see that something flickered in his eyes at the movement. His mouth thinned to a slash of tension.

'Don't do that,' he flung at her.

Miranda jumped, confused.

He drew a long breath, visibly drawing on reserves of control. Slowly he sat back on his heels and surveyed her.

'Listen to me, Miranda. I don't know what you've been told about me. The gossips make up their own rules. But I assure you, you have nothing to fear from me,' he said with great deliberation.

It was like an icicle plunged into her heart. She did not move, did not say a word, waiting for the pain to subside.

He put out a hand and tilted her chin. 'Do you understand me?'

Pride came to her aid.

'You mean you won't seduce me,' Miranda interpreted with bravado. She gave him a glinting, defiant smile. 'Not very complimentary. But in the circumstances I suppose it's quite reassuring.'

He stared at her, his eyes narrowed.

'As you said, I'm not a fool,' she pointed out, turning the icicle dagger in the wound. 'I know it's a reassurance you wouldn't give me if I were a halfway attractive woman.'

He expelled a short explosive breath. He cursed again in his own language. 'You don't have much of an opinion of my morals, do you, Miranda?'

She looked him full in the eyes. 'I form my judgements on the basis of the evidence,' she told him.

His eyes flickered again. He gave a harsh laugh. 'Evidence you've gathered yourself?' he mocked.

Miranda flushed.

'And I thought I was behaving impeccably,' he went on in a derisive tone. 'I even warned you, if you remember.'

Her flush deepened. Her eyes fell under the burning contempt in his. She did not understand that contempt but it flung itself at her as inescapably as the wild wind outside.

'Then God forbid that I should try to sway you against the evidence.' Paul sounded icily furious. 'After all, who better than an untouched adolescent to sit in judgement of me?'

He came lithely to his feet. Miranda looked up at him, startled. There was something in the swift, elegant movement that spoke of stark purpose. It alarmed her. She shrank away from him as he towered over her in the deepening shadows.

Quick as a snake he put out a hand and hauled her to her feet. She stumbled over the beautiful rug in which her feet tangled. Paul paid no attention at all. He was staring down at her, his eyes hooded and brooding.

'You have no idea, have you?' he said in a harsh, bitter whisper. 'No idea at all.'

'W-what do you mean?'

'The needs of ordinary mortals,' he said, his mouth twisting. 'Not outcasts. Ordinary human beings. The normal, human instinct for a little warmth, a little comfort. It's all black and white, villains and saints for you.'

Miranda was scared at the storm she seemed to have raised up unwittingly. But she was no coward. She glared into his angry eyes.

'Just because I believe the evidence of my own eyes...'

'Then here's some more evidence,' he said in a goaded voice. 'Believe this.'

He dragged her the last few inches over the crumpled rug and fastened his mouth on hers in a punishing kiss.

CHAPTER NINE

IT SHOULD have been frightening. In a way it was. But stronger than the fear there was the undisguisable hunger. For both of them.

Miranda registered it, even as her hands tangled in his hair and she strained against him. Paul made a sound that was almost a groan.

'I must be losing my mind,' he said in a husky whisper. '*Miranda* ...'

His hands at her waist were like a vice. She shivered. His mouth was travelling languorously along her jaw, the length of her arched throat. She felt as if her whole body was turning to him, like a plant to the sun, opening to him.

She sighed. Paul's hands tightened. With a slight, delicious shock she felt his teeth nip gently at the tender skin below her ear. She groaned in her turn. It was a deep contralto sound she would never have recognised as her own.

When I told Maria Clara I wanted adventure, I never thought of this, she thought exultantly. I thought I wasn't going to have anything more to do with love. What a fool I was.

She sought his mouth with her own.

This kiss was longer and fiercer. When Paul broke it, she had to hold on to his shoulders to keep herself upright in a reeling world. His body was like a rock, steadying her.

'Miranda, I——'

Her eyes were dazed. 'Kiss me again,' she invited softly.

He swallowed. She saw his throat move. 'Oh, God, if only...'

'I want you to.'

He expelled an abrupt breath. His mouth tilted wryly. 'I know you do. But——'

Miranda put the back of her hand to his cheek. 'Kiss me. Please.' She moved against him. He closed his eyes briefly.

'You don't know...' he began raggedly.

'Then teach me.' The gentle invitation was more than half a challenge.

She looked at him from under lowered lids. She saw him register the challenge. And react to it. His mouth twisted bitterly.

'I'm no tutor for an innocent. You know that as well as I do.'

He put her away from him with an effort and stepped back. Miranda stared, not quite believing that he could do it.

'Don't look at me like that,' he said explosively. 'Oh, God, Bebel was right.'

Miranda went very still. 'Bebel?'

Paul was almost talking to himself. 'She even warned me. You may be twenty-three but you're a child in experience. Only a villain would take advantage——' He broke off.

Miranda said evenly, 'How am I going to improve my experience, then?' This time it was pure challenge.

Paul met her eyes, startled. What he saw there made him say something savage under his breath. He kicked at the crumpled rug, sending it spinning into a corner.

'I shouldn't have kissed you, I know. But——'

Miranda thought she had never felt so hurt in all her life. She took refuge in anger. Glaring at him, she demanded accusingly, 'Is this an apology?'

His eyes flickered. He went very still. For a moment she thought he was going to touch her again. She held her breath in an agony of expectation. His expression froze into a mask. But then suddenly he gave a soft laugh.

'No. Villain I may be. But an honest villain. I don't apologise for what I enjoyed.'

'*Enjoyed*!' It was a trivial word for what she had felt; for what she'd thought she had sensed in him as well. She searched his face for evidence that she had not been deceiving herself.

He withstood the inspection impassively. One dark eyebrow flicked up. He said, as cool as ice-water, 'Something for you to remember, missionary's daughter. Men enjoy kissing beautiful girls.'

Miranda rode it like a blow. She was shrewd enough to see that he wanted to make her retreat from him. It still hurt. But there was her dignity to think of.

'Thank you,' she said with ironic sweetness. 'I promise to remember.'

'Consider it my contribution to your education.'

This time, thought Miranda, it sounded as if he wanted to hurt himself as much as her. It was no comfort.

'Remind me to arm myself before any further educational exchanges,' she retorted.

Inside she was hurting badly. I love this man, she thought. How on earth did it happen? We have nothing in common. He thinks I'm a child. I *know* he has no conscience. He says as much himself. We have nothing in common. We're only together because of the floods. When the river falls he'll send me away and be relieved I've gone.

Yet all she wanted to do was go into his arms and kiss away those lines of cynicism, the heart-deep loneliness she sensed in him.

She folded her hands together hard. She was not going to admit any of that to this sarcastic, smiling man. She might love him, but she was not a fool. It would not do her any good at all to tell him she loved him.

Paul said wryly, 'I think we could both do with some armour. I'd forgotten——' He stopped abruptly.

Outside the wind rose to an ominous roar. The long drapes at the window stirred like ghosts. Miranda shivered.

'Don't look like that,' Paul said. 'It sounds like the hounds of hell, I know. But it will pass.'

Another huge gust hit the side of the house. The table lamp rattled. Its uncertain light sent the shadows streaking up the wall like long devilish fingers reaching for their victim.

Miranda shivered again. She had never felt so scared, she thought. Or so lonely. If only he would hold her.

But he was on the other side of the room now. And he looked as if he was going to remain there.

She tried to smile. 'Will it?'

'Yes. And then the river will fall and you can go back to civilisation and get on with your life.'

She bit her lip. 'It's a long time since I've lived in "civilisation" as you call it. I don't know how I'll take to it again after all these years.'

The handsome face was calm, remote. 'You'll enjoy it.'

'Will I?'

'Of course. You've missed a lot in the last five years. Not just an education... Company of your own age. Pretty clothes. The Disney *Beauty and the Beast*.' His tone was determinedly light. 'You've got a lot of catching up to do.'

Her smile was edged with pain. 'More education, Paul?'

He seemed to go very still. Then he said, 'Call it advice. From someone who knows the world better than you do.' He straightened his shoulders. 'You need to spread your wings. Have fun. Experiment a little. It's what you're entitled to.' His voice was level. 'But not with me, Miranda.'

There was absolute silence in the room. Even the howling wind seemed to have fallen. Miranda thought she could hear herself breathing. She wished she weren't.

She had thought she was hurt before but this... She would much rather be dead, she thought remotely.

But there was still the frail escape route of pride.

'Of course,' she said. She hardly recognised her voice. It sounded as if it had been packed in ice through several milleniums.

Paul said something under his breath. The anger in it was raw. Miranda flinched from it, though she could see that the anger was directed at himself as much as her.

Then he drew a breath and said without expression, 'You don't believe me now, I know. But you will one day.'

'Maybe.'

He took a hasty step towards her, then stopped.

'Not maybe. Certainly,' he said with determination.

She shook her head. 'I know more than you think,' she said drily. 'Why do you think I came away with Harry in the first place?'

Paul's eyes narrowed. 'Some adolescent affair that went wrong does not exactly constitute vast experience.'

All of a sudden Miranda was angry, really deeply angry. She met his eyes.

'You really do think you know the answers to everything, don't you?' she said quietly. 'Well, in this case you're wrong. I was young, yes. But not stupid. I had a boyfriend who said we were going to get married. I—wasn't happy in my uncle's house. After my mother died no one really wanted me there. I was lonely. Keith made me stop feeling lonely. But that didn't mean I lost my grip on reality. He said we would get married. I believed him.'

Paul's eyes were expressionless. 'So what happened?'

Miranda sighed. 'He was very young too. I didn't realise I should have allowed for that. His family weren't well off. They had this wonderful old house that was falling round their ears. My cousin Claire was the one with the big trust fund. So——' She shrugged.

It had seemed so important at the time, she thought wonderingly. The end of her world. Now she could hardly remember what Keith Ware looked like.

'He married your cousin?'

'Yes.'

'And you took off for the Amazon jungle?'

Did he sound ever so slightly scornful? Miranda lifted her chin proudly.

'I took off for the Amazon jungle, as you put it, because I was living in the same house and Keith did not see why we couldn't continue our—involvement. On a strictly private basis, of course.'

The bitterness she had felt showed in her savage tone. She drew a shaky little breath, calming herself deliberately.

'Did Harry know?'

Miranda shook her head. 'Nobody knew except Keith and me. And now you.'

He was very still.

She said painfully, 'There was no one to tell. My mother was ill for years before she died. So I sort of perched with uncle's family. Never quite at home. Always expecting to move on. It didn't make for the ideal background to form relationships.'

Paul said with feeling, 'You don't need to tell me. There were times when I lived in a different town every week when my mother was on tour. Then my father decided to pay for my education and I was sent to the States to school.' He looked at her shrewdly. 'So that's what you were looking for from Harry Lane. Stability. Affection.' His expression was not unsympathetic. 'Didn't get it, did you?'

Miranda bit her lip. She did not answer. There was no need.

Paul gave an explosive sigh. 'Lord, what a mess. And this is all you've got to go back to in England?'

She looked away. 'Yes.'

A curious expression crossed his face. 'I wonder if Bebel can have been wrong after all?' he murmured. But before Miranda could demand an explanation, there came a terrific crash.

'What was that?' she gasped.

'One of the trees in the garden, at a guess.' Paul touched her arm very lightly, withdrawing his hand at once when she turned to him. 'None of them is going to fall on the house. My grandmother planted very carefully with that in mind,' he said, his voice strained. 'We're quite safe. It will have blown itself out in the morning. Why don't you go to bed and forget it?'

Miranda shivered. 'Forget it?' she said incredulously as the net curtains billowed, in spite of the protection of the wooden shutters.

Paul grinned suddenly. 'Yes. Not a very bright suggestion on my part. All right. Why don't you sit down and I'll give you a drink?'

She did so. Paul went to the drinks tray and came back with a pale drink that tasted of limes and cinnamon.

'Tom Collins,' he said briefly when she asked what it was. 'It's not strong but you'd better treat it with respect all the same. Tell me, do you play chess?'

Miranda shook her head.

'Draughts? Cribbage? Scrabble?'

Suddenly she was angry. 'I'm not a child. You don't have to take my mind off the danger of the storm.'

His eyes glinted. 'How do you know it isn't my own mind I want to distract?' She stared at him. 'And there are more dangers around tonight than the wind,' he added deliberately.

Miranda winced. 'I wish you wouldn't say things like that,' she said after a moment.

'Don't you like the truth, Miranda?' It was a taunt.

She met his eyes. 'I don't like being played with,' she said quietly.

At once his expression was shuttered. 'I'm sorry,' he said formally.

She sighed. 'Tell me how you came to set up your research project here,' she said, searching for a neutral subject.

Paul looked at her disbelievingly for a second, then he gave a soft laugh. Miranda raised her head alertly. It was not a pleasant laugh.

'You mean will I confirm the rumours?'

'What——?' she began, not understanding.

'Very well,' he said. 'I'll tell you. What you heard was the truth. My grandfather left me the *fazenda* because he thought my father's family owed me something.' He paused and then added harshly, 'In spite of the fact that I seduced my sister-in-law.'

It was such a shock that for the first few seconds Miranda thought she could not have heard right. She stared at him blankly.

He gave a bark of laughter. 'It wasn't like your Keith. You don't have to look like that. I didn't want an affair behind Tomas's back. I was young and idealistic then. A lot like you are now. I wanted to marry her.'

Miranda was still getting her breath back. 'Only the young and idealistic marry?' she said at random.

He laughed again but differently this time, as if she had really amused him.

'*Touché*,' he said wryly. 'Though I think it would take someone exceptionally unwary to want to marry Bianca.'

Miranda was not deceived by the rueful tone.

'What was she like?'

'Enchanting—but not kind to her suitors. In fact part of her charm was that they never knew where they were with her. One day she was all melting compliance—the next she'd look straight through you if you met at the beach.'

Miranda swallowed. Smiling had never been so hard, she thought.

'And you were a suitor?' she asked with commendable lightness.

His face was sombre. 'For a while.'

Until Bianca chose Tomas, presumably.

'And she did that to *you*?' Miranda hated the way she sounded, unconcerned and as mocking as Paul at his coolest. 'Looked through you on the beach?'

'Particularly on the beach.' His smile was cynical. 'I was very definitely not for public display.'

Miranda clenched her hands in her lap. He would not have liked being a lover in secret, ignored in public. He would have *hated* it. To put up with it, he must have been very much in love.

'What happened?' she asked when she had command over her voice.

Paul shrugged. 'We met in my room at the university mostly. She wasn't married then, of course. Not even engaged. I used to think——' He bit it off.

Miranda said nothing, though her nails were digging into her palms so hard, she could feel the blood pulsing against the pressure. He must have been so hurt, she thought.

He shrugged again, then resumed. 'Well, I was wrong. She was never going to marry me, whatever she said. Sometimes we went up into the mountains. I had a friend who had a chalet there. He'd let me borrow it for weekends. Bianca had to have an alibi, of course. She used to say she was going to see her grandmother. The old lady was so confused, she never knew whether Bianca had been or not.' His mouth moved in distaste. 'Not pretty, is it, missionary's daughter?'

'No,' Miranda agreed quietly. 'Was that how you were found out?'

'No.' He sounded almost surprised. 'No. It was much more ordinary than that. She got engaged. To my half-brother.' He paused. 'My legitimate half-brother,' he added. His voice sounded as if he had been dragged over gravel.

Miranda felt a wave of fury that was as unfamiliar as it was unexpected. He would have been so *hurt*, she thought, wincing.

'Don't——' she said in a suffocated voice.

'You asked.' He was pitiless. Watching her, he added negligently, 'You might as well know the worst about me after all.'

She turned her head away.

'I tried to talk her out of it,' Paul said, his eyes dark with memories Miranda could only guess at. 'Tomas was rich and good fun and would give her everything she wanted. We could go on seeing each other, she said. In fact it would be easier when she was a married woman with no one to question what she did with her time. Tomas wouldn't care because he wouldn't know.'

Miranda shook her head. It all sounded horribly familiar. They were exactly the arguments Keith had used.

'You turned her down?' she said almost pleadingly.

'I tried to persuade her not to marry him.'

From the look on his face, there was not much doubt about the shape that persuasion had taken either. Miranda felt sick. How in love with her he must have been!

'It didn't work. So then I told Tomas. Men in love are blind. He didn't believe me.' He smiled. It was not a pleasant smile. 'So then my grandfather took a hand. He was a shrewd old bird. He knew more about Bianca than either of us. He brought Tomas to my apartment one evening when Bianca was there.'

Miranda could imagine it with a vividness she found terrible. She did not want to ask for any details.

'Unfortunately, he reckoned without that blindness I spoke of. Tomas rewrote the evidence of his own eyes. I was the villain, of course. The vile seducer who couldn't keep his hands off the misguided poor little rich girl.'

'What happened?' asked Miranda, sickened.

'Oh, I was thrown out.' Paul sounded indifferent. 'Berated for ingratitude. Banished from the family. That didn't matter. My father stopped paying my postgraduate fees. That was a nuisance for a time. I worked my way through, though, one way and another. And when my grandfather died he left me the estate. As compensation, his will said.' His face was bleak.

'You were in love with her,' Miranda said slowly. 'Weren't you? If you sank all your principles like that, it wasn't just sex. You were in love.'

He looked at her with a curious expression. 'Principles?' he said in an odd voice. 'What makes you think I've got principles? I thought the godly had me down as the devil incarnate?'

Miranda stiffened her spine. 'I don't take my judgements from other people. I've known you less than a week but I've seen you in more than one crisis. With other people depending on you, too. You don't *behave* like the devil incarnate.'

His eyes narrowed. 'And that's your considered judgement?'

She tilted her chin. 'Yes. And I trust it.'

'Judgement?' Paul Branco said softly. 'Or instincts?'

Miranda knit her brows, bewildered.

He sat down and leaned back against the velvet upholstery. His hair was very black and the tanned jaw uncompromising. In spite of the dust and the torn shirt, he looked impossibly handsome. He was watching her from under lowered lids. Something about his expression made her heart lurch suddenly.

'Believe me,' he said lazily, 'you would be most unwise to trust your instincts where you and I are concerned.'

Miranda jumped. Her skin felt suddenly cold. He had not touched her. He had not moved. But she felt as if he had laid a hand on her shoulder and turned her to stone, and that she would stay stone until he brought her alive again with another touch.

Her heart began to beat high and hard somewhere up in her throat. The silence stretched between them. Miranda felt cold and hot at the same time. Fearful and yet excited. Conscious that she was on the brink of some crucial choice; something that would change her whole life.

She held her breath, looking at him. And, even as she watched, she saw him withdraw into himself. It was as if one moment he was there in the room with her challenging her with every lazy, laughing word, then, as if he remembered something terrible, his eyes darkened and he just was not there any more.

He seemed to be lost in thought. Memories, Miranda concluded painfully, called up by their conversation. The handsome face looked infinitely remote. In spite of what he'd said, he had forgotten she was there, Miranda thought.

She studied him. So here, she thought, was the source of that terrible loneliness she had always sensed in him. Her name was Bianca. She had cost him his family and very nearly his education and she still haunted him. Miranda's heart twisted in her breast as if she had been stabbed.

There was another, closer crash. It earned a small scream from Miranda and brought Paul out of his reverie. It was followed by a terrifying rushing noise.

'I'm sorry,' she said, recovering herself.

He was on his feet. 'You're entitled,' he said briefly. 'The next room, I think. Stay here.'

He ran lightly from the room. Miranda hesitated only a minute before following him.

It was more than a shutter. A fierce gust had torn out a whole French window, taking a good part of the surrounding woodwork with it as well. One shutter had gone completely. The other lay on the floor. But even as Miranda stared, in horrified fascination, it was sucked out of the hole in the side of the house. As if a dragon were licking it up, Miranda thought.

She had to put her full weight against the door into the passage to close it. She could feel the strength of the wind pulling at her too. She gave a small exclamation. In the din made by the wind it was impossible that Paul should hear. But he turned his head and shouted something at her.

Miranda could not make out the words. She shook her head, going closer to him.

'Get back,' he shouted above the wind. 'Go over to the other side of the house.'

But Miranda was staring past his shoulder. She put out a hand to steady herself against him. Instinctively, it seemed, his arm went round her, holding her safe.

'There's someone down there,' she shouted back.

'What?'

She pointed to where the skeleton of a fan-shaped traveller's-palm was bending to the ground in the path of the wind. Underneath it, huddled but unmistakable, was a figure. It seemed to be wearing a red headscarf—incongruously frail protection against the lashing downpour, Miranda thought.

Paul saw it too. He swore. A savage gust pulled at them again. He staggered and the arm round Miranda tightened. The tumbled furniture converged on the broken window in a sinister rush.

Beyond the window the traveller's-palm was nearly horizontal. It seemed impossible that the crouching figure could survive the savagery of the elements.

'We can't just leave him there, whoever he is,' Paul said. He sounded furious.

Miranda clutched at him. 'Don't go out there. You'll be killed.'

'I'll be careful.'

'*No*!'

'I have to,' he said as he had said to her before. 'There is no one else.' He measured the distance with his eyes. 'It's only a couple of hundred yards. There's a rope in the stables that will stretch that far. I'll tether myself.'

Miranda's hands were frantic. 'What can you tie yourself to?' she shrieked at him, as the furniture made another eddy and the door to the passage shook ominously. 'Don't go. What's the point in two people being hurt?'

Paul did not answer. Instead he fought his way back across the room, taking her with him. He dragged open the door to the passageway and almost forced her through it. He was breathing hard.

'Go to my study,' he said curtly. 'It's out of the direction of the wind. You'll be safe there.'

Miranda's mouth set in stubborn lines.

'I'm coming with you.'

He gave a little laugh that cracked. 'My darling, you can't. The wind would have you over in a trice.' He stroked wild strands of brown hair off her face as if he could not help himself. 'Anyway there's only one rope.'

'Then I shall hang on to the end of it,' Miranda said.

Paul shook his head. 'You're not strong enough. I need to tie it to one of the main house supports.'

'I'm not leaving you to do this alone,' Miranda told him firmly.

He gave her a curious look. But all he said was, 'Very well, then. You can stand guard and make sure the rope holds. Well out of the wind,' he added with a firmness that equalled her own. 'Meanwhile stay here and don't move.'

He was back inside five minutes with a heavy coil of rope. He looped it round his waist and tied it in a competent knot. Miranda looked on with misgiving.

'What on earth can you tie it to? Everything in that room is moving as if it's on skates,' she said caustically.

Paul gave a soft laugh. 'A challenge indeed.'

Miranda glared. 'You're enjoying yourself,' she accused him.

His eyes glinted. 'I enjoy challenges. So do you.' And he tweaked her nose. 'Don't you?'

It annoyed Miranda so much that she turned away from him. When she looked round again he had attached the rope to the central pillar at the foot of the staircase and was testing his knot.

'This is going to be a nuisance because it means that we won't be able to close the door properly. So you'll have to put your whole weight against it, keep it shut as much as you can, until I get back.'

Miranda forgot her annoyance. She felt the blood drain from her face. In the shadows Paul could not have seen it but he touched her shoulder reassuringly.

'In ten minutes it will all be over. Come on. Fling yourself against that door the moment I'm through it.'

Before she could protest, he was through it and tugging it closed behind him. She had no option. She did as he said.

It was the longest ten minutes of her life. She could not see her watch. The hallway was in total darkness. The wind outside sounded like a wild animal. All she could do was push with all her might against the door and pray that Paul would be safe.

It went round and round in her head like a prayer: Please, please, *please*.

And then, Don't let me have found him only to lose him now. Before I've even told him I love him.

Miranda caught her breath at the sudden realisation. Oh, she had thought she loved him before, she had told herself she loved him—but she had not meant this wholeness, this absolute confidence, this trust. She had still been too wary, remembering the shallowness of Keith Ware's professed love, the non-existence of Harry's, once she had returned to Brazil with him.

But Paul was not like that. He did not say what he did not believe. She gave a little laugh, remembering how he had told her he did not make promises in bed or out of it. With a man of Paul Branco's integrity, Miranda thought, you did not need promises.

She gave a deep sigh. In spite of the turmoil on the other side of the door, she felt a great peace sweep over her.

She tipped her head back against the majestic wooden door and smiled.

'All I have to do now,' she said wryly to the carved staircase; 'is tell him.'

CHAPTER TEN

MIRANDA had no more time for reflection, however. The noises beyond the door were no longer those of the storm alone. She stood away from the door and braced herself to hold it open just wide enough to admit Paul. He was carrying what looked like a limp bundle of washing over his shoulder and he was bent nearly double against the wind.

As soon as he was through he flung his back against the door and he and Miranda forced it shut. Then he turned and tipped the bundle slowly forward.

It was a woman—a girl not much older than herself, Miranda thought. She looked as if she had been rescued from the sea rather than a storm. Her eyes were closed and the red scarf had been soaked to black.

'Rubem's Elena,' Paul said wearily. 'She goes to him while he's busy going to her. God preserve me from the insanity of lovers.'

Miranda flinched a little at that, but it did not seriously disturb her lovely serenity.

'I'll look after her,' she said, supporting the semi-conscious girl. 'Go and get into something dry before you catch pneumonia.'

He grinned. In spite of his drenched and muddied state, in spite of the physical feat he had just accomplished, he did not look weary. He looked wickedly alive. Meeting his eyes over Elena's head, Miranda felt her heart begin to thunder.

'Yes, madam,' he said with mock-meekness, and ran as lightly down the darkened corridor as if he had just come in from a gentle stroll.

Miranda took Elena to the kitchen and poured hot, sweet tea into her until the girl came to her senses. At first she was bewildered, then frightened for Rubem. But as soon as she was told that he had taken the truck to her own village where no doubt he was now safely waiting out the storm, the Brazilian girl succumbed to exhaustion.

Reluctant to use the upper storey in case the roof was damaged, Miranda installed the girl in one of the makeshift beds in a room off the kitchen. Elena, she saw, was asleep before Miranda was out of the door.

And Paul?

Miranda hesitated. He wanted her. She had no doubt of that. He had told her as much. And he had never attempted to disguise his feelings, no matter how strong a curb he had tried to impose on his expression of them.

Oh, yes, he wanted her all right. But he thought she was too inexperienced to know her own mind; that anyone who tried to make love to her now would take advantage of her innocence. And Paul Branco had principles. He would not come to her, no matter how much he wanted her.

So it's up to me, thought Miranda. She shivered a little. The boldness of the idea now presenting itself to her was alarming.

Are you a coward? she said to herself fiercely.

Well, yes, maybe a little. After all, she had never made love with anyone. And Paul knew it.

Do you love him or don't you?

That was the crux, of course. And there was no question about the answer. So there was no real question either about what she was going to do next.

Miranda went back to the drawing-room and retrieved one of the oil lamps. She turned the others out. As she did so she looked down at herself ruefully. The rain had not soaked her as comprehensively as Elena or Paul but her clothes were still sticking to her unpleasantly.

She risked a quick return to her bedroom, where the rafters were shuddering, and scrambled out of her clothes. Then she pulled on her borrowed silken robe and, fastening it tightly round the waist and taking up the oil lamp, went forth to seek her fate.

She knew where the master's room was, although she had never entered it. She went downstairs and along the corridor to the big corner room. She opened the great door softly. There was no light, no sound. Paul did not seem to be there.

Miranda closed the door and raised her lamp. She stood very still, her eyes darting round the darkly shadowed room. Nothing. She fell back against the door, trying to still the agitated beating of her heart.

What if she was wrong? What if he did not want her after all? Or not want her enough. What if he threw her out? What if he refused to take her seriously?

She loved him, Miranda reminded herself. She needed to tell him so. Maybe she could save him from whatever demons drove him. But whatever happened, no matter how fearful she was, she knew she could not walk away from this.

She pushed away from the door and walked across to the curtained bed. Her bare feet made no sound on the polished boards. The naked flesh beneath the robe felt cold.

You love him, Miranda repeated to herself fiercely. She wrenched back the hangings.

Paul, lying very still in the middle of his bed, contemplated her without expression. The laughing eyed hero of an hour ago had disappeared entirely.

Miranda met his implacable gaze. She swallowed. Then, very carefully, she put the oil lamp down on the bedside table.

She stammered, 'I—I didn't hear you. I didn't think you were here.'

Paul was unsmiling. 'Didn't you?'

He had got rid of his boots, the soaking breeches and the dark linen shirt. He had replaced them with disgraceful jeans, stained and dusty. He was not wearing a shirt. Miranda shivered again.

'No. I——'

He had his hands linked behind his head. The tanned skin rippled over powerful muscles. His hair was very black against the exquisitely laundered linen. He did not move from the bed.

'What are you doing here, Miranda?' he asked quietly.

She moistened her lips. He watched her do it, his dark eyes unreadable.

'I—er——'

'Well?'

She swallowed something hard in her throat. Get a grip, she told herself fiercely. This needs a sensible answer.

'I thought you might like help,' she said, improvising rapidly.

'Help?' he echoed softly. It was a softness she had never heard in his voice before.

'Taking your boots off.' She knew it was ridiculous. She knew she babbling. She felt horribly embarrassed but ploughed on, 'I thought you might like me to do it. If you're tired, I mean. And bring you a drink maybe. You like a drink when——'

'When my resistance is low,' Paul agreed. He was wry. 'Well, as you see I managed to remove my boots unaided. And——' he nodded at the heavy mahogany table by the bed; there was a bottle of rum on it '—I am well-provided with the necessary comforts.'

His voice was level. He sounded completely unmoved by her presence. Miranda felt the hated colour rise in her cheeks and looked away.

'Can't we talk?' she said at last.

'What subject did you have in mind?' he said drily.

Miranda's invention gave out. Her colour deepened.

He moved suddenly. At once Miranda tensed, her heart racing. His look of irony deepened. Slowly and deliberately he swung his legs to the other side of the bed and stood up.

They stood facing each other, the great curtained bed between them. As if they were enemies, she thought, astonished. His eyes were as dark as a forest pool in the storm—and about as welcoming, Miranda thought.

'I don't think I want to know what you're doing here,' Paul said. 'It doesn't reflect well on either of us.'

Miranda searched his face and made a discovery. In spite of the determined lack of expression, he was not as indifferent to her arrival as he wanted her to think. There was a pinched look about his nostrils as if he was holding himself in check only by a very great effort.

Some of the embarrassment began to seep out of her. Courage returned, and with it curiosity. What was putting that look of strain on the handsome profile? She walked slowly round to his side of the bed. The beginnings of a smile tugged at the corners of her mouth.

'If you know why I'm here, then I don't need to tell you,' she pointed out softly.

His eyes flickered, but they did not look away, she saw.

'Don't play games you don't understand, Miranda,' he said, suddenly harsh.

She stopped by the ornate carved bedpost. She looked at Paul thoughtfully. If he put out a hand he could touch her. He put his hands swiftly in his pockets. But not before she had seen that they were clenched, the knuckles white with tension.

She put her head on one side. 'Games, Paul?'

He swore softly and virulently.

'Go back to bed, Miranda.' She shook her head. 'I don't want you here.'

His eyes were hot. There was no doubt, she thought, that he was very angry. But there was more in that taut body than anger. Miranda needed to know how much more.

The need was suddenly pulling at her like the force of the storm outside, of gravity itself. She put a hand to her throat. Her very skin seemed to be shaking under the impact of that planetary magnetism. It was stronger than her fear of his anger, stronger than natural modesty or all of Harry's careful precepts.

She made a swift instinctive move towards him. His head went back as if she had hit him.

'God, what does it take?' Paul swore, his eyes suddenly blazing.

Just for a moment Miranda quailed. Seeing it, he took a hasty step forward.

'Get out. You don't know what you're doing. Just get out.' He made an almost violent gesture in the direction of the door.

Miranda could see that he meant it. His eyes were molten with anger.

Fortunately, her legs were trembling so much, she could not have moved even if she had wanted to, Miranda thought with irony. She took hold of the bedpost to steady herself. She thought with sudden absolute clarity, He's channelling everything into anger so he doesn't have to look at what else he's feeling.

He was so clearly torn apart by her presence that she wanted to take him in her arms and tell him she wanted him as much as he wanted her. She did not—quite—dare.

'Don't,' she whispered.

'I mean it, Miranda. Get out. Now.'

She shook her head, clinging like a monkey to the supporting bedpost. The flimsy robe stirred with the rapid rise and fall of her hurried breathing. She saw Paul's eyes skim the shadowed softness of her breasts. For a moment she felt as if she was never going to breathe again.

'Miranda.' It was a groan.

She shook her head quickly. 'Don't send me away.' If only she did not sound so young and scared, Miranda thought in despair. She didn't feel young and scared. Not with Paul looking at her like that. She felt wholly adult. 'Please don't.'

She closed the gap between them and set her hands on the strong bones of his naked shoulders. She strained to look up into the handsome face. Even through eyes swimming with tears, she registered his expression. It was stark desire. It was almost shocking in its bitterness... and its need.

So she had made the right choice after all, Miranda told herself, blazingly exultant all of a sudden. No matter what he said, she was right to follow her instincts.

She stood on tiptoe and slid her hands round his neck. Slowly, slowly she brought the handsome head down to meet her. Paul felt like stone in his resistance. His mouth was compressed into a slanting slash of tension and his eyes were implacably blank. But there was nothing he could do to disguise the way his heart was slamming where her body pressed against his own.

Miranda gave a soft laugh of pure joy. She felt her lips part and soften as she brushed them, very gently, against his own. Just for a moment she felt his hungry response. She gave a long sigh and melted against him.

'*No!*'

He tore himself away almost violently.

Shocked, Miranda staggered. She collapsed, or Paul half flung her—she was not sure which—on to the side of the huge bed. She put her arms out to brace herself. Head bent, she drew great gulps of air into her lungs. She felt as if she had been climbing a mountain and, all of a sudden, had lost her footing and fallen into the depths of a canyon.

'What the hell do you think I am?' He flung it at her like a challenge.

Miranda shook her head, bewildered. 'I don't understand.'

'So you've woken up to sex and decided to experiment.' Paul drew a long breath. 'Fine. You're on your

SAVING THE DEVIL

way back to civilisation. Wait until you can find a boy of your own age.'

She stared at him. 'It's not an *experiment*,' she said, shocked. 'I may not have your experience but I can still control my instincts. I'm not a fool, Paul. I——'

'That's nonsense,' he interrupted harshly. 'Intelligence has nothing to do with it. Nobody can control their instincts, Miranda. *Nobody*. Believe it——'

'But——'

He ignored the tentative interruption. 'All that civilised people can do is put a brake on the way they behave. And only then if they can catch themselves before they go out of control. You can't control your feelings, Miranda.' He sounded bleak. 'All you have a chance of controlling is what you do about them. Sometimes. If you see them coming. If you're lucky.'

Miranda stared at him.

Suddenly savage, he said, 'It doesn't help if beautiful girls whose brains haven't caught up with their bodies come and throw themselves at you when you're——' He broke off. But he had already said enough to give himself away. Miranda's eyes widened. She sat suddenly straighter.

'You *do* want me,' she said on a note of discovery.

Paul swore under his breath. Miranda ignored it. She stood up.

'You do, don't you?'

'Don't use me to practise your wiles on,' he said in an ominous tone.

She ignored that too. She took two steps forward. 'You can't give me a lecture about honesty and then refuse to tell the truth yourself,' she said softly. 'You want me.' She met his eyes, daring him.

His face tightened. For a timeless minute they stood in the shadowy room, not touching, not even within touching distance, locked in a silent combat. Outside the storm howled. The light of the oil lamp flickered wildly at the gusts which buffeted the house. There might have been only the two of them in the whole of the universe.

At last he said very quietly, 'Yes, I want you.'

It did not, Miranda realised with a startling *frisson* of awareness, sound like an admission of defeat. And she did not feel like a victor, although she had wrung that admission out of him against his will. Instead it took all her self-control not to retreat before the look in his eyes. Her heart began to flutter as if she was afraid.

I'm in love with him, she reminded herself.

He trod silently towards her, making no noise on the polished floor. Miranda watched him. She felt mesmerised, like one of the small jungle rodents facing a predator. Facing, she thought shakily, its fate.

'Oh, yes, I want you,' he said again. 'I'm a man. I've done my experimenting. When I see what I want I know it.'

Miranda gasped.

He was coming closer, like a stalking panther. There was no kindness in his face.

'I knew I wanted you from that moment in the tent. You knew something was happening but you didn't know what it was all about then, did you? That was before you had woken up to the possibilities. Before you elected me your—tutor.' The quiet tones were raw.

Miranda shook her head violently. Paul took no notice. His hands shot out suddenly and she was hauled towards him in a movement that made her alarmingly conscious of the fragility of her body. There was no kindness in his hands either.

He looked down at her. 'I'm no teacher, darling,' Paul told her cynically. 'If you come to me, you come as an equal. And take the consequences.'

Miranda's eyes squeezed shut at the onslaught on her quivering mouth. No kindness and no concessions to the inexperience he was only too ready to remind her of. He lifted her as if she were made of paper. He held her against him in a caress that was explicitly designed to demonstrate the gulf between their respective experience.

Miranda gasped. She tried to remember that she loved him. But all she was aware of was the strength and the anger in the arms that held her.

Suddenly she was free. She opened her eyes. She felt dazed.

'Game getting too serious?' Paul taunted. He watched her face. 'That's the risk, Miranda. The problem with this game is that you can choose what you start but you'll be damned lucky if you can choose anything else after that. Those instincts that Harry should have told you about take over. Your instincts, Miranda. But mine too. So no more experiments, please. For the peace of mind of both of us.'

She repeated achingly, 'It was not an experiment. I *love* you.'

'For God's sake.' His voice ripped out at her. 'Am I to be spared nothing?'

She retreated involuntarily a couple of startled steps.

'Go to bed, little girl,' Paul commanded. 'Go to bed and stay there, thanking God that I let you go alone.'

He took hold of her chin and forced her to look at him. His face was devilish for a moment, stripped down to naked need. She saw the need, the bitter self-reproach and the anger all at war in him.

She said in a shaken whisper, 'I want you to be *happy*.'

His mouth went rigid. 'No more pretty glosses, Miranda. You want me to take you to bed,' he said brutally. 'I've warned you——'

She flung back her head and looked him straight in the eye.

'Yes, you've warned me and warned me. But you've never told me what would be so terrible about making love to me,' Miranda cried passionately.

'Love?' The bones of his face were suddenly harsh, as if the flesh had melted away leaving only the suffering essence of the man. He took two steps towards her. 'Love?'

Insolently, almost idly, he pushed the robe aside. He ran one fingertip over her—over the fragile ridge of her collarbone then lifting each breast in turn, then, so slowly she thought she would die of the waiting, down the silken sweep of her stomach and down again, parting her thighs with barely a touch.

Their eyes met like opponents. His face was quiet without expression. His fingers were suddenly fierce. Miranda heard herself gasp. Her head fell back and she clung to him. For a few wild seconds she was conscious of nothing except the whirlwind he was driving into her, through her. It was as if he had ripped away the camouflage from her most secret self and was bent on making her, naked, scale heights she had always known were there... and been deeply afraid of.

She cried out, shuddering, eyes screwed tight shut. There was a long silence. The remorseless hand was removed.

'Curiosity satisfied?' said the harsh voice at her shoulder.

Miranda opened her eyes slowly. She was afraid of what she was going to do. But the fear was nothing compared with the fear that he might send her away and she would never see him again. She shrugged herself out of the robe. It pooled round her feet on his floor in a splash of ruby. It was the only colour in that muted room.

Briefly Paul's expression was unguarded. He looked tortured. Then he stepped away from her. A muscle worked in his cheek. His eyes swept her up and down in one comprehensive glance. He was determinedly unmoved. Except that Miranda could see the slight unsteadiness of his breathing and knew he wasn't unmoved at all.

She lifted her chin, forcing him to meet her eyes. She pushed back her hair with fingers that trembled. He made no move. She stepped out of the pool of silk and stood in front of him. He made an involuntary movement, abruptly stilled.

Their eyes locked. Something told Miranda not to touch him again; that the next move must be his.

In a silence like the end of the world, she retreated to the bed. She lay down, looking at him all the time. She thought he closed his eyes briefly, but in the uncertain light of the oil lamp she couldn't be sure.

He came to the bed on silent feet. He looked down at her, his face still.

'I tried to send you away.'

'Yes,' she agreed softly.

'If I could be sure you understood what you're doing...' He sounded as if he was talking to himself.

'I understand,' she said, shaking her head. 'You told me, remember? "I don't make promises. In bed or out of it." It made an impression on me.'

The grooves beside his mouth were suddenly as deep as they had been when he was in pain.

'But did you believe it?'

'Yes.'

'And you still want—to be here?'

There was a silence so taut, Miranda felt she would shatter. She shut her eyes.

'I want to love you,' she whispered.

'So be it, then,' he said with murderous softness.

Her eyes flew open. But he was already beside her on the bed. For the first time in her life Miranda felt the shadow of his mighty shoulders lowering over her and the soft heat of his mouth on her flesh, unaccustomed to such attention.

He kissed her everywhere, slowly. He made no allowances for her inexperience or her shyness. When his passion startled her, he laughed softly. When she jumped and protested, he silenced her with kisses that made her senses swim. And he laughed at that too.

This was not what she had expected, Miranda thought confusedly. All her fantasies of a gentle giving of herself were burning up in the fire of that slow, calculated passion. For he never, not for a moment, lost control of himself or her. If there was a point to be made here, it was not the power of her love but the dark, irresistible force of his own practised sensuality. Even as she writhed under his touch, Miranda was shocked.

She had been so sure she could give him love. So *sure*. Yet the giving here was all on his side. And she didn't think it was love. Miranda had never imagined these sensations, never thought herself capable of the little animal moans that seemed to be coming from another throat a whole universe away.

'No,' she groaned.

But it was too late. Already his hand was sweeping down her limbs in a gesture of absolute possession. With vast astonishment, she felt her body shift, accommodate itself to his. From a great distance, she saw that this was the point of no return.

She knew she was afraid. She tried to tell him. But his body was urgent now. She tried to say his name. She wasn't sure she made a sound. He didn't hear. His breathing was thunderous suddenly. She cried out in alarm. He hesitated then—too late.

Miranda had not expected pain, hadn't thought about it, even. This agony was all the more frightening because of that carelessness. She felt as if Paul had flung a thunderbolt at her and she had splintered under the impact. Every nerve reverberated with the shock of it.

She fell back, her breathing harsh in the silence and more eloquent than any exclamation of pain could have been.

He touched her face. His eyes were not unreadable any more. They were full of anguish.

'Oh, my darling.'

His fingers touched her cheek as if they were afraid to shatter her. He made to withdraw.

And suddenly Miranda was not afraid any more. Suddenly all the love she had been so sure of flooded through her again. Suddenly everything was wonderfully, gloriously right.

She slid her hands across the breadth of his shoulders and drifted her mouth over that harsh jaw, clasping her to him, welcoming him with all her strength.

'I love you,' she whispered with absolute assurance.

And he lost that immaculate control at last.

The wind had finally fallen when Miranda woke up. It was still dark, though. For a moment she did not know where she was.

She knew the body lying next to hers, though. She knew the curve of his shoulder under her cheek and the steady rise and fall of his breathing. In the half-daze before she came fully awake, she thought they were back in the forest in the claustrophobic tent, and that he did not know she was a girl. She tensed.

'Miranda?' Paul's voice was very soft, but it was not sleepy.

Nor, she thought sadly, was it husky with love. She shifted a little, so that their bodies were no longer touching.

'Yes?'

Miranda felt the movement in the pillow as he turned his head to look at her. He did not try to touch her. She felt him looking at her in the darkness. Her whole being cried out to him to touch her, to take her back to his arms; to tell her he loved her. He did not.

Instead he said carefully, still in that midnight whisper, 'How do you feel?'

What am I supposed to say to that? Miranda wondered sadly. I'm in love with a man who feels nothing for me; am I supposed to feel wonderful?

'Fine.'

He was very still. Then she thought he gave a small sigh.

'I tried to tell you.'

Tell her that he did not love her? He hardly needed to tell her that. His every word, every action did it for him.

'You did.'

There was a short, painful silence. *Hold me*, Miranda cried silently.

'I didn't expect the regrets to set in this quickly, I confess,' Paul said with sudden harshness.

Miranda shut her eyes tight against the pain. He was regretting it already? She clamped her lips together to stop herself begging him to take her in his arms again. What price dignity now?

She swallowed. 'I'm sorry.'

He hauled himself up on one elbow in an abrupt movement and leaned over her. Miranda opened her eyes. She was profoundly grateful for the darkness. In the shadows Paul was looking at her intently.

'"Sorry" is a bit of an understatement by the looks of it,' he said drily. He was not whispering any more. He touched her face gently. 'Don't break your heart, little one. All things pass in time.'

She fought down the thickness of tears in her throat. 'I'm sure you're right. This is just—so new to me.'

'That's the trouble,' he agreed. 'And not new at all to me. The gap between us is too wide. I'm sorry, my darling.'

The endearment was the last straw for Miranda's precarious self-control. Her bottom lip began to tremble. She looked wildly round for her robe.

'Miranda——'

It was his arrogant voice, the one in which he had barked instructions at her in the forest. Miranda sniffed surreptitiously and did not turn.

'I ought to look in on Elena. Last night she was——'

'Very wet and very tired,' Paul interpolated. There was an undertone of unmistakable laughter to his voice. 'She won't thank you for waking her up. Let the poor woman sleep. We have things to discuss.'

Like how quickly Bebel could get the helicopter to collect her, Miranda thought drearily. She bent her head.

'Do we?' She sounded sulky, like the child he so often called her, she thought despairingly.

He looped her hair behind her ear absently. The tender possessiveness of the gesture tore at her heart. If only he cared. But she had never asked him to care. She had wanted to give, not to bargain, and that was exactly what she had done.

He said thoughtfully, 'Why did you come here last night, Miranda? Apart from helping me to take my boots off, of course,' he added ironically.

In the darkness of the morning, she felt the hot colour storm into her face at the reminder.

'You know,' she muttered at last.

'I thought I did.'

She shrugged, keeping her face averted. She thought she heard him sigh.

There was a creak and Paul swung himself out of bed. He crossed to the great shutters and threw them open, first on one wall, then the other. Light flooded in. Miranda blinked, screwing her eyes against the sun's assault.

He turned and surveyed her, magnificently unconcerned at his nakedness. Miranda gathered the linen sheet to her breasts protectively. As she grew accustomed to the light she saw that Paul was looking at her with a smile lurking at the back of his eyes.

Forgetting her own embarrassment, Miranda stared in amazement. The look of strain was gone. In its place had come a dancing mischief that made him look as if he had been released from prison. She hardly recognised him.

'Now, why?' he said quite gently.

He seemed to be looking right through her to her soul. Miranda looked round for that robe again, her breasts rising and falling in agitation.

'Or shall I tell you?' Paul suggested lazily.

She swallowed, not looking at him.

'I think I made a mistake about you, didn't I, Miranda?' he said in a musing tone. 'In fact we all did. You should have heard the lecture I had from Bebel about your youth and my lack of it.'

That startled Miranda sufficiently that she forgot not to look at him.

'From Bebel?'

Paul's smile was crooked. 'We may not be lovers,' he said deliberately, 'but she's a shrewd woman and a kind one. She could see how it was with me. She thought it was unfair to you. She was very worried about leaving you here with me, to be honest. She only agreed because she could see I wanted to—care for you if Harry was dead. As we both thought he must be.'

Miranda shook her head, bewildered. 'You wanted to care for me? But you didn't know me. You *can't* have done.'

'But I did,' Paul corrected softly.

'B-but——' she stammered. The look in his eyes made Miranda's head swim. 'Paul——'

Paul came back to the bed. He walked round to her side and sat down, taking Miranda's hands in both of his. He held them strongly.

He said with great deliberation, 'Frankly, my darling, it never occurred to me that I would fall in love again. It hadn't done me much good the first time. And it would never have occurred to me that a woman like you even existed—let alone that I would fall in love with her.'

Miranda began to tremble. This time the endearment did not make her wince. She cleared her throat.

'What do you mean—a woman like me?'

'Gentle,' he said. 'Brave. Funny. Innocent. God help me, so innocent, it was like walking through a minefield. You see, I'm not innocent. And I knew the dangers. I tried to warn you. But all I did was frighten you at first and then——' the familiar crooked smile twisted his mouth '—well, you weren't frightened last night, were you? More determined to prove your point than scared, I thought.'

Miranda nodded. 'Yes,' she admitted. She lifted her chin bravely. 'Look, Paul, you don't have to be kind to me. I know what I did last night and it wasn't your fault. I threw myself at your head.'

He lifted her hands to his lips and kissed her knuckles lingeringly. 'Yes, you did, thank God,' he said with feeling. 'I was having a bad time battling between my instincts and my scruples.'

He opened her fingers and pressed his lips to her soft palm. Miranda closed her eyes. A little shudder of pure ecstasy went through her.

'Well, I've admitted it. I was in love,' Paul murmured, that note of amusement still in his voice. 'What's your excuse?'

Miranda's eyes flew open.

'*Oh*!'

She pulled her hand away.

He repossessed it easily. 'Well?' He might sound amused but there was more than laughter in the dark eyes. 'You still haven't answered my question.'

'Qu-question?'

'Why did you come to me last night?'

Her eyes fell. He would not allow that. He took her chin, quite gently, in his fingers and made her look at him.

'I should have listened to you, not Bebel. You're right. You're not a child. You know what last night meant. To both of us,' he told her softly.

Miranda flushed, her eyes filling with sudden tears. Paul put a finger very gently under each eye to blot them.

'I have never met such honesty,' he told her quietly. 'When you make love you give your whole heart, don't you, my darling? That was no experiment last night. That was love.'

Miranda sat very still. She was tongue-tied.

'Is it so difficult to say? Will it help if I tell you I adore you? That I fell hopelessly in love from the first moment I saw you, in that ridiculous hat, trying to pretend you were an urchin? That I never want to live without you again?'

She found her voice. 'But Bebel—you were in her room,' she said.

She remembered their caress with painful clarity. Although, with the evidence of last night to guide her, Miranda had to admit that in retrospect it had not looked like a passionate caress. She knew, now, how Paul kissed a woman in passion and that was not how he had kissed Bebel.

Paul held her away from him and looked down at her. The handsome face was suddenly sober.

'I won't lie to you, my darling. When I first came here—well, Bebel was new to the job and lonely and we were both outcasts in our own way. She thought she was in love with me for a while. I was never in love with her. I know loneliness when I see it and I know the difference between that and love. I told her so. And since then she has been in love with Heitor do Campo; she knows it for herself.'

'Heitor?' said Miranda wonderingly. 'So when you seemed so distracted and worried about her when you both got back the other day, it was because Heitor was injured. Oh, what a fool I've been. I thought it was because you were lovers.'

Paul shook his head. 'Bebel is a friend. The only lover I have—or want—is you, God help me, suspicious and headstrong though you undoubtedly are.' He gave her a little shake, his eyes dancing. 'Now are you going to marry me or aren't you?'

Miranda's eyes widened until she thought they would explode. 'You can't marry me,' she said, dazed.

'Yes, I can,' Paul said calmly. 'Neither of us is already married. All I need is your consent. And,' he added wickedly, 'I now know how to get it.'

Miranda blushed. She could feel herself beginning to smile. The warmth was spreading through her like sunshine after the storm.

'You said you didn't make promises, in bed or out,' she reminded him mischievously.

Paul groaned. 'Suspicious, headstrong and possessing total recall of every unwise remark I've ever made.'

'Well?' said Miranda, bracing herself against his chest and meeting his eyes limpidly. 'Didn't you mean it?'

'I meant it,' he said. 'And marriage to you isn't a promise. It's a necessity.' Suddenly he was very serious. 'After you fell asleep last night, I realised that you had to have come to me because you loved me. No other reason. You didn't care what other people said about me.' He held her hard against him. 'And you already knew me better than anyone had ever done. In a few short days, you realised that I was not a callous Lothario, that I had truly loved Bianca. You tell the truth, my lovely Miranda. And you see very clearly when other people tell it too.'

His lips moved against her hair with sudden passion. She basked in his arms.

'I need you in my life,' Paul said quietly. 'Marry me, Miranda. Stay with me forever.'

She gave a long sigh and lifted her face for his kiss. 'Yes,' she said simply.

His face blazed with such happiness that she blinked. Then, realising that it must mirror her own expression, she smiled deep into his eyes and said what she had wanted to say last night and not dared.

'Hold me forever, Paul. Love me.'

'I will,' he said.

A Book Designed to be Given...

A collection of creative, unusual and wonderful ideas, to add a spark to your relationship–and put a twinkle in your eye.

A Handbook for Men
A Godsend for Women

Why be romantic? Why bother?
Simple. It's inexpensive, easy–and lots of *fun*!

Available January 1995   Price: £4.99 (Hardback)

Available from selected bookshops and newsagents.

Look out for Temptation's bright, new, stylish covers...

They're Terrifically Tempting!

We're sure you'll love the new raspberry-coloured Temptation books—our brand new look from December.

Temptation romances are still as passionate and fun-loving as ever and they're on sale now!

MILLS & BOON

Next Month's Romances

Each month you can choose from a wide variety of romance with Mills & Boon. Below are the new titles to look out for next month, why not ask either Mills & Boon Reader Service or your Newsagent to reserve you a copy of the titles you want to buy – just tick the titles you would like and either post to Reader Service or take it to any Newsagent and ask them to order your books.

Please save me the following titles:	Please tick	✓
TRIAL BY MARRIAGE	*Lindsay Armstrong*	
ONE FATEFUL SUMMER	*Margaret Way*	
WAR OF LOVE	*Carole Mortimer*	
A SECRET INFATUATION	*Betty Neels*	
ANGELS DO HAVE WINGS	*Helen Brooks*	
MOONSHADOW MAN	*Jessica Hart*	
SWEET DESIRE	*Rosemary Badger*	
NO TIES	*Rosemary Gibson*	
A PHYSICAL AFFAIR	*Lynsey Stevens*	
TRIAL IN THE SUN	*Kay Thorpe*	
IT STARTED WITH A KISS	*Mary Lyons*	
A BURNING PASSION	*Cathy Williams*	
GAMES LOVERS PLAY	*Rosemary Carter*	
HOT NOVEMBER	*Ann Charlton*	
DANGEROUS DISCOVERY	*Laura Martin*	
THE UNEXPECTED LANDLORD	*Leigh Michaels*	

If you would like to order these books in addition to your regular subscription from Mills & Boon Reader Service please send £1.90 per title to: Mills & Boon Reader Service, Freepost, P.O. Box 236, Croydon, Surrey, CR9 9EL, quote your Subscriber No:................................ (if applicable) and complete the name and address details below. Alternatively, these books are available from many local Newsagents including W H Smith, J Menzies, Martins and other paperback stockists from 13 January 1995.

Name:..
Address:..
................................Post Code:........................

To Retailer: If you would like to stock M&B books please contact your regular book/magazine wholesaler for details.

You may be mailed with offers from other reputable companies as a result of this application. If you would rather not take advantage of these opportunities please tick box. ☐